LUNATIC
RUTHLESS ASYLUM BOOK ONE

K.L. SAVAGE

COPYRIGHT© 2021 LUNATIC BY KL SAVAGE

All rights reserved. Except as permitted by U.S. Copyright Act of 1976, no part of this publication may be reproduced, distributed, or transmitted in any form or by any means, or stored in a database or retrieval system, without prior permission of the author. The scanning, uploading, and distribution of this book via the Internet or via other means without the permission of the publisher is illegal and punishable by law. Please purchase only authorized electronic editions and do not participate in or encourage electronic piracy of copyrighted materials. This book is a work of fiction. Names, characters, establishments, or organizations, and incidents are either products of the author's imagination or are used fictitiously to give a sense of authenticity. Any resemblance to actual persons, living or dead, events, or locales is entirely coincidental. LUNATIC is intended for 18+ older, and for mature audiences only.

ISBN: 978-1-952500-28-2

LIBRARY OF CONGRESS CONTROL: 2020924724

PHOTOGRAPHY BY WANDER AGUIAR PHOTOGRAPHY
COVER MODEL: TUG JAMES
COVER DESIGN: WANDER AGUIAR
EDITING BY: INFINITE WELL
FORMATTING: CHAMPAGNE BOOK DESIGN

FIRST EDITION PRINT 2021

To our crazy readers,
Thank you for making this book possible. The Ruthless Universe has grown so much because of all of you and this book wouldn't have come to life without our readers, so thank you from the bottom of our hearts.
Please keep in mind that this book is a work of fiction, but the meaning behind loving hard is not. There are a lot of people in the world who are afraid to love and to feel loss because sometimes it hurts like hell. Don't be afraid to love hard to the point where it is crazy and consuming (safely) and give that person every ounce of effort you have.
Love lives everywhere.
Even in the Asylum.
Even for the minds that aren't all there.
Love. Is. Maddening.
With or without a mental illness.

PROLOGUE

Zain

Ten years old

THEY ARE GOING TO FIND ME.

They are going to kill me.

And there's nothing I can do. There is no escaping them. There are so many of them. It's impossible to win.

"They're coming," I whisper, staring out the window and watching the sky.

"No one is fucking coming," Martin, my big stepbrother, snaps. "You're insane. You keep thinking they are going to come out of the sky and get you. No one is fucking coming, Zain. Jesus, enough already." He flops onto the bed and untwists his headphones that are tangled in a nest. "Will you get the fuck out of my room? Chelsea is on her way back with Jesse."

"You would say that because they aren't coming for you!" I yell and tap against the window to the black sky with all the flashing lights. "They are there. They want me! Why aren't you listening to me! Why doesn't anyone ever listen?" I cry, feeling the panic grip my heart. "They want me to be their leader. I'm not ready." I ignore his order to leave the room. I don't want to be alone. I want to be right here, where I know I am safe.

My stepbrother rolls his eyes and covers his ears with his headphones, then blares rock music to tune me out. Everyone tunes me out, but my parents always listen to Martin. He can do no wrong, and it's because he is the next in line to have the MC handed down to him. Stupid Legacy crap. I never understood the meaning behind it all.

My brother is twenty-one and got a girl pregnant seven years ago. While it wasn't responsible for a fifteen-year-old to get his girlfriend pregnant, they kept the baby. He's grown into a six-year-old boy who runs around without a shirt and likes to steal my stepdad's cut, since he is in charge of the Ruthless Kings.

The kid's name is Jesse. He is my nephew, which is weird since we are only four years apart. Well, step-nephew. We don't have any blood shared, which is probably why I'm the outcast, the unloved one, the outsider. My blood is no good. At least, that's what momma says.

Martin could have six kids and my stepdad and momma would be so happy. Because all of them would be normal. They wouldn't be freaks.

They wouldn't be a disappointment. They wouldn't be me.

LUNATIC

But not *them*. They want me.

I bring my thumb to my mouth and chew on the nail. Maybe I don't need to be afraid. They named me their leader for a reason. I need to be there. I can do it. I can be who they need me to be.

I grip the sides of my head when the noise becomes too much and begin to rock back and forth. "Stop, please. Make it stop!" I scream at the top of my lungs. "Why doesn't anyone listen to me?"

The door bursts open, and I jump back. My mom is standing there with a grim look on her face, but one that's more annoyed than worried. "Can't believe I got stuck with a dud for a kid," she says, smacking me upside the head. "It wasn't even that bad of a fall. You didn't hit your head that hard. Snap the fuck out of it," she yells, slapping me again.

"Momma, they are coming for me," I say, tears filling my eyes. "They want me there. We need to go. We have to move." I hook my hands in my mom's shirt, desperate for her to listen to me. I don't see the threats, but I know what they want.

And they want me.

"You know what, Zain? I'm going to be happy when they take you away," Momma says as two men wearing white uniforms come through the door.

One has a syringe in his hand. "Momma, who is that? Who are they? They came for me, didn't they? I won't let you take me!"

I try to run around them, jumping over the bed, but my foot catches on the edge of the mattress. I tumble to the floor, smashing my face against the hardwood, and my arms are pulled behind me as something wraps around my wrists. It's tight, hard, and feels like the plastic that my toys are made of.

"They found me," I whisper. "There is no getting away from them. You guys have to leave! Please leave."

"I can't wait until I'm no longer responsible for you," Momma says. "You're too much to bear, Zain. You're too much of a burden. You aren't normal."

"Momma, I am. I am, normal. I'm telling you. Look, they are taking me just like I said they would! Momma, look. You have to believe me. Please," I sob, tugging on the restraints as hard as I can, but I'm trapped. The room starts to spin, and I lose my footing, tripping over my left foot. One of *them* saves me from smashing against the ground. I want to be thankful, but if they want me with them, why do they need to restrain me? "Dad?" I whimper when I see him at the door. It's wide open, and the humid air makes it hard to breath from the heat. "Dad, don't let them take me," I beg.

"You need help, kid," he says, slapping a big hand on my shoulder. "You'll realize it one day."

What are they saying?

I don't understand.

When the sun hits my face as they push me out the door, I see a van waiting in the driveway. My heart is pounding in my chest. It's like the better part of me is dying to get out, but the bad side of me is too strong. I can't fight it.

This happens sometimes. I have really high highs and

low lows. I don't understand it, but it's so hard for me to focus sometimes because of how fast my mind is running. It's gotten me in a lot of trouble at school, but I don't know how to control it. It's like I suddenly wake up and they tell me what I did wrong.

"Where am I going? What's happening?" I start to come out of the fuzzy haze that's fogged my mind when they try to put me in a van. "No. No! I'm not going. You can't make me go." I struggle, lifting my legs to kick and scream.

"Kid, let them help you!"

"Coming from you, that's means nothing!" I shout to the man I once thought of as my new dad. Tears drip down my face when I read what's on the side of the van.

Nevada Psychiatric Facility.

Where minds come to heal.

"I'm not crazy. I'm not!" I scream louder until my throat is raw.

No one is listening to me.

I kick my feet up and they land on the fender. The men grabbing me don't expect it, and I use my small size to my advantage. I push out, letting my feet press against the side of the van. Their grips loosen and I yank out of their hold and dart away.

I try to run back inside the house where my family is, one of the few places I've called home, but my mom is there is the doorway, and she slams the door in my face. A sharp pinch hits the back of my arm and when I look, I notice a dart of some sort.

My head turns foggy again, and I spin slowly, wondering

how two grown men can drug a ten-year-old-boy. Another tear drops down my cheek when I realize what's happened to me. They're the only family that I've ever known. Sure, my momma bounced around before settling with the President of the Ruthless Kings. I had always wanted a brother, so when I met Martin, I thought I had it all.

The only person in that house that loved me was Jesse, and he didn't know me well enough to hate me yet.

I'll miss the little guy. He was my buddy.

"I got ya," a stranger says as I fall, and before I can hit the ground, he catches me in his arms. "I'm sorry you have to go through this. I really am."

I believe him.

He sounds sad for me.

He shouldn't waste his breath. I'm not worth it.

The van door slides open, and I'm placed in the backseat. It's leather, smells like my brother's gym bag, and it's hot.

He shuts the door at the same time I shut my eyes. I give up. I'm not going to fight anymore. Fighting has gotten me nowhere in life. Hopefully when I wake up, I'm somewhere where I feel more like myself, and maybe one day I can come home again—when I'm better.

If I'm better.

Only time will tell.

I know I'm only ten years old, but I feel like I've lived a hundred lives with all the energy in my mind. It's constant electricity. I can't shut it off.

And I don't know if I will ever be able to.

LUNATIC

Thirty-five years later

"Happy Birthday, Zain," the guard says, banging the baton against the door. "How many years does that make it? Thirty?"

Thirty-five. He's close enough. It's been a long fucking time and guess what? I'm going to get the fuck out of here today. I'm done living my life behind bars. Apparently, my stepdad and mom died, leaving a shit ton of money to Martin, only for him to fucking die too.

The bastard of course paid for me to stay for so long, I'd die here, and my soul would be taken care of behind these bars.

I ain't a bad guy. I just want out. I can prove that I can be worthy to the world.

"Jesus, you've been here longer than I've been alive, you know that?" Huck, the guard, taunts through the small speaker in the window.

I ignore him the best I can and continue to do my push-ups. If there is one thing this place has offered me, besides drugging me up, it's the chance to work on my strength. They keep my head in a fog, so I don't have manic episodes, but I'm done feeling like a zombie.

I'm ready to release what's been buried inside for over thirty years.

"Hey, I'm fucking talking to you, crazy-fuck," the guard

says, swiping his card across the scanner. The door buzzes to allow him in and his boots thud heavily, getting closer and closer until my chin hits the tip of the leather. "Can you not understand me? Are you stupid too?" he asks, trying to rile me up.

I've been a damn good patient here in this fucking cage, but you know what? I'm tired of feeling like a pet. I'm only fed when I'm allowed, and when I'm told to heel, I have to. Years ago, I made a plan. Years ago, I learned the layout of the property when I had my walks. Years ago, I learned the inside of the building like the back of my hand.

I've been working myself up, building strength, because I know more guards will come, and I need to be able to take them down.

I've only known one man to escape the facility, and that's Porter. He said he'd find a place for us to live, but in order to get there, I have to call the number at the bottom of the letter. I will when I get out, and this time, I'm not going to pull a Porter.

I'm going try and take as many with me as I can. No one deserves to be locked up, beaten, and starved, just because we are a little different.

I'm tired of taking medication every day that makes me so numb, I can hardly remember what I had for breakfast.

Huck lifts his boot and the rounded tip of the leather presses under my chin. "I'm talking to you. I won't say it again," he says.

I freeze mid-pushup and close my eyes as the rapid thoughts invade my mind. The familiar manic energy starts to pump, but it's muted from the medication. I only stopped taking it a few days ago. Considering how long I've been on it, I'm going to assume it's going to take some time to get it all out of my system.

Do I want to keep taking the medication? Maybe, but in smaller doses. I haven't decided yet.

The musky leather of his shoe invades my nostrils. I can smell the strong fumes of polish and the dirt on the bottom of his shoe. "You're too fucking close if I can smell the shit you stepped in outside," I say, keeping my voice level and calm.

I'm too fucking old to get too worked up. Forty-five will do that to a man, especially when he has been in a cage for most of his life.

The baton replaces his boot. At first, it's colder against my skin before warming to my temperature. "What did you just say?" he sneers.

I grab his baton, sweat dripping in my eye and stand to my full height. I yank the weapon from his hand, staring down at him as he looks up at me. Yeah, I get that a lot. People think they are so big and bad outside these walls, but once they are in here with me, they change their tune. "I said, I can smell the dog shit on your boot." I plunge the baton into his gut, then whip it up and slam him in the face. Blood spews from his mouth, along with a tooth, and the red liquid spatters along the tile.

"You're in so much trouble."

"No," I grunt, kicking him onto his back. "I have twenty minutes before anyone comes looking for you. You're the one in trouble." I squat down and press the baton against his groin. He's young, but he is a real fucking asshole, and I don't know what to do with him. Maybe I should kill him and be done with it.

He smiles, his white teeth stained red. "You're never going to get out of here. I'll make sure of it." Huck reaches into his pocket to pull out his radio.

Aw, that's cute.

I slam the baton on his hand next and the bone crunches. Before he can make a noise of pain, I grab his neck and twist it. The sick crunch sends shivers down my spine. His pupils dilate, getting larger until all that remains are black pools of death.

Tugging his bent neck forward; I bring his ear to my lips. "Watch me," I whisper. I pick him up and place him in my bed, then cover him up with the thin sheet they give us to sleep on. I tug the keys from around his belt buckle and steal his keycard.

I hold his keycard in the air and examine it, then stifle a laugh. "Bucklebee Huck? You poor bastard. No wonder you were an ass. You were compensating for your shitty name." I tuck the keys into my back pocket and walk away, ready to leave this shithole behind me. Better yet, just to be safe, I turn around and pick the baton up off the floor. It reminds me of what cops wear on their hip. The guard isn't even supposed to have this. They aren't allowed to abuse the patients here, but this facility is what nightmares are made off.

No one cares about the patients, their mental health, or their physical health. This place can go to hell for all I care.

LUNATIC

They want to try to cage insanity?

Let's give them a taste of what happens when it's set free.

I swipe the card over the scanner and the large metal doors swing open. I step out, crack my neck, and groan with relief. That spot has been bugging me for a while now.

"Zain," my friend Apollo says with excitement from the room next to me. "Get me out of here, man. I need my books. I need to study my work and art. Oh, how I miss music, Zain. Please, set me free." They think I'm crazy. This fucking guy believes he is Apollo, the Greek God. He's a good guy, though. He's been my friend for ten years. His family dumped him in here just like mine did.

"You don't even have to ask, Apollo. That was my plan all along." I swipe the card and his door swings open automatically.

He bows to me, then follows me down the hall. I don't know if Apollo thinks he is truly a Greek god, or if he has a personality disorder. I don't know too much about what they diagnosed him with. All I know is what they say about him.

We're all crazy.

We're all dangerous.

We're all wastes of space.

I run down to the next door; the soft soles of my shoes barely make a noise. The next room we get to is Marigold's. She's lying in the bed, her back turned to us. She has a major depressive disorder. I've never seen her smile, but we play checkers together. She's become a good friend. "Goldie," I call out, using the nickname I gave her five years ago. She has long blonde hair, so it makes sense. "Goldie, come on. We are getting out of here." I look left and right to make sure we are still in the clear. We have fifteen minutes before we need to worry.

She turns slowly to me, and when she sees me and Apollo, her eyes smile even if she doesn't. "Zain?"

I slide the card on the scanner and open the door. "I'm breaking us out."

She doesn't question me. She bolts out of bed, scurrying to the doorway. She wraps her arms around her waist and stares at the floor.

"We have to hurry," I tell them, and we still have a few people to get out. I won't miss these long hallways, white tiles, and bright lights.

Apollo wraps an arm around Goldie and hurries her along. She trusts him to guide her forward because she hates to look up. She hates to look at her destination or the people in between. Goldie is always lost in thought.

"Felix, let's go!"

"Do you see them?" he asks, looking up frantically and darting his eyes around the room.

"See what?" I ask impatiently.

"The dragonflies."

"Oh, that's nice," Apollo says, staring above Felix's head in envy.

"Pretty. Oh, so pretty, Felix. Let's go. We need to get Oli." I press the card against the scanner and Felix comes running, swiping at his head.

LUNATIC

Then he ducks and shuts the door, pointing at the fake dragonflies. "Ha! You're trapped."

I grab his wrist and pull him along. For a second I'm wondering what the hell I'm going to do with a bunch of diagnosed crazies like us, but I'll figure it out. We don't deserve to be here.

When we get to the last door, Oli is there, counting his steps. "Make a wish, set it free, and if it comes true, it was meant to be," he says three times. Oliver has an extreme case of Obsessive Compulsive Disorder. His compulsions are in three.

"Oli! We need to get out of here."

"Zane! Hi. Hi. Hi."

"Hi, Oli. Come on, we are leaving." I swipe the card one last time for my friend that always gave me his applesauce because he knew I liked it so much.

"I like trips. Where are we going? Hi. Hi. Hi." He waves to Apollo. "Hi. Hi. Hi." He greets Goldie next.

I'm happy not everything he says is in threes, or we would be here all damn day. Right as he walks out, the alarms sound and the locks start sliding into place.

"Fuck," I curse.

Lockdown.

If we don't get out of here in the next few minutes, we are going to be trapped.

"I don't have time to hold anyone's hand. We have to run, so you better keep up." Without giving my friends another look, I start to run down the hallway and pump my arms. There isn't time to jog. We have to sprint.

"Hey! Stop right there!" A guard shouts from behind us.

"Oh, no. Oh, no. Oh, no," Oli chants as he sprints by me, a crazed, panicked look on his face.

I grab him by his shirt and hang a left down another hall. "Follow me, don't pass me, Oli."

He nods, sweat beading down his red face.

The guard's boots pound on the tile behind us, echoing the madness living in these walls. We get to another door, and I slide to a stop. Just beyond this door is our promise of freedom. But I have to take care of the guards first. "I want you guys to run, okay? Run as hard, and as fast as you can. I'll catch up," I say, gasping for breath as I see the first guard round the corner.

"We aren't leaving without you," Goldie says, sad and forlorn with a quiet voice.

"I will be fine. I promise," I squeeze her shoulders and watch as big metal bars clink across the doors as the lockdown makes its way to the end of the hall.

Right where we are.

I slam my body into the door and open it. "Go! Now!" I yell at them as the sun bears down on my shoulders. I'm afraid they aren't going to make it. I grab Oli by the shirt again and throw him outside. "I said, go!"

They run out the door, one by one, and I lift my elbow to smash a guard in the face at the very last minute. I lay the baton between the crack of the door so it doesn't shut all the way, in hopes I can still get out of here.

Another guard comes, waving a taser in the air. He presses the sides and a blue bolt sparks between the two metal tongs. I slide left and miss the electricity by a hair, grab his arm, twist it, snap his wrist, and press the taser against his neck. His body shakes and jerks from the electricity, collapsing.

The loud clanks of the locks stampede down the hall with each metal bar. There are only a few doors left before I don't have time to make it out. A guard's fist connects to my face. Blood slides down my tongue like a tasty drink. A chuckle escapes me, and when he tries to hit me again, I catch his fist and plunge the taser in his gut. His body quivers just like his coworker, but the difference is he bites his tongue and blood tints the inside of his lips.

"You will not abuse my mental illness, or my friends more than you already have." I press his body against the wall and hold him by his throat.

"You'll never make it out there," he wheezes, then laughs, coughing as the blood chokes him. "You'll kill people. You people aren't capable of living a normal life."

The bars locking the door slide across the doorway, and the force of the lockdown system pushes the metal so fast and hard, that it cuts right through the guards body. He's locked to the wall, impaled just like the door is supposed to be. I jerk my head up from the bar in his torso when I hear more boots thudding in the distance.

"Yeah, looks that way, doesn't it?" I say, patting my hand on his pale cheek. I duck under the rod, grab the baton that kept it cracked, then use my shoulder to push it open. "You're going to want to put a band-aid on that. And don't forget…" I grab his chin, not giving a fuck about the blood marinating down his mouth, "...to take your medication for that," I say, throwing the words of this place back at him.

I dip out the door and it slams shut behind me. The Nevada sun barrels down on my face and I run toward the woods, putting this nightmare behind me once and for all. I've spent more than half my life in this hell hole.

And I'm done.

"You okay? You're bleeding," Apollo asks as I catch up.

I stare down at the cuts across my knuckles and nod. "Yeah, I'm good. We need to hurry. Porter said to call him when we get to a safe place." We all start running through the woods, the distant yell of guards in the background along with the bark of search dogs.

Whatever happens, the effort is worth it.

I want to experience something other than the chaos inside my mind. Something more than being trapped, confined, and hated in a place that hates the mentally ill.

I don't care if this world kills me, because I've been dying slowly for the last thirty-five years.

CHAPTER ONE

Zain

Present day

I SWEAR I HEAR THE SCREAMS OF THE PAST HAUNTING THIS PLACE. The low groans of people fighting their minds resounding down the hallways. Their pain forever soaked into the rotten walls of this Asylum.

I guess that's why it feels so much like home. Is it sad that the surrounding vintage of what used to be a mental institution brings me comfort? I suppose it shouldn't, considering I killed two men to get out of that hell hole.

This hell hole is mine. That's the difference.

We're all sleeping on the floor right now. No blankets. Just huddled on the floor against each other to keep warm. We don't have a lot of money right now, but we will. I'll figure out a way to take care of everyone. I have to. I'm the only one mentally capable enough to hold down a job.

Which doesn't say much, does it? But it was my idea to bail us out of the Asylum, so this is on me to take care of my friends. They left a place where at least they could rely on a bed and three meals a day, to come with me to a place with a leaky roof, holes in the floor, and crumbling walls.

The only new things we have are the clothes and shoes we stole from a retail shop on our way here to meet Porter, but that isn't going to be enough to get us by. The clothes will get dirty and how are we going to wash them?

Fuck.

I'm in over my head. I shouldn't have brought them here.

"Zain. Zain. Zain." Oli's repetitive nature has me blinking, looking away from the catastrophe of the living room. Oli is sitting in one of the rusted wheelchairs he found down the hallway, trying to roll it closer to me, but the wheels are stuck from old age.

"Hey Oli," I greet him with a smile and rub my temples when an ache starts to throb. The feeling of restlessness starts to enter my body.

"Have you been sleeping well?" Oli asks, tapping the armrest of the chair three times. "You know you have to sleep, Zain. You have to sleep for your mania."

"I know, Oli. It's been a little stressful, that's all. I'll be fine."

"Porter has been asking for you," Oli informs me.

"I don't care, Oli. He's lucky he is still alive, and for all

I know, that won't last long." I kick a piece of drywall into the fireplace and a cloud of smoke and dust billows out. I place my hand on my hips and take a look around this dump Reaper graciously let me rent from him. I know he bought the place out of spite because he knew Porter was living here. I'm not sure what's going to happen. The entire situation is a shit show.

The only reason Porter is not torn to pieces right now is because of Tongue.

His half-brother.

And while I don't know how that is possible, I have to be grateful, because at the end of the day, Porter has been my friend longer than the rest of the gang has. I've seen him when he's normal, pumped full of medication to keep him 'Porter' and not this 'Groundskeeper' he keeps insisting we call him.

He isn't a bad guy. He just needs help.

But I'm not going to throw him in a mental institution. We deserve to be in a place where we are cared for, surrounded by friends, love, and laughter. We deserve a life.

Reaper's condition was that we hire a nurse to keep us in line, but I can't afford to yet. I told him we had one in order for him to rent us the place, but that was a lie. I was desperate for us to have somewhere to be.

I won't give up my friends like the system gave up on us. They shoved us away in a cold, dark corner. We weren't wanted. The people we needed tossed us out like trash. They hated us for being different, for being more than what they were used to.

And we were left to die.

I'm not standing here saying I'm a good man. I know I'm not. I killed two people, and I don't feel bad about it. I did what I had to do for my family. My friends might not be like everyone else's, but they are mine.

They are my makeshift family of misfits, and as long as I have them, I'll be okay. Don't get me wrong, I'd give anything for Reaper to want to get to know me, but I'm just a stranger to him. A man who is sick in the head. A man who Reaper's father gave up on. I'm nobody to him, and he shouldn't have to worry about getting to know me. There isn't any pressure.

But he gave me a photo album for Christmas, full of the years I've missed of his life. I haven't stopped looking at them. I must open the album thirty times a day. Reaper is a better man than his old man ever was, I can see that. The only thing I can hope for is he gives me time to prove to him I'm not unstable and worthless.

I can be something.

I can be someone.

Somehow.

Feeling eyes on me, I turn over to look over my shoulder and everyone is staring at me.

I swallow and the rusty wheels of the chair Oli is sitting in squeak, grating my nerves. I rub the back of my neck, the energy surging. I'm becoming restless. I need to speak. I need to say something.

"Iknowyouguysarelooking—" I raise my voice, needing them to hear me, but speak fast. I have to speak fast or what I need to say won't come out.

Goldie lays her hand over my mouth. "Breathe," she says, inhaling and exhaling slowly for me to follow. "You're talking too fast and you're sweating. Stop now before you get yourself too worked up and you're in bed for three days." Her voice is calm, like one of those voices you'd hear on sleep meditation.

I need to do something. Maybe I can fix the staircase, or I'll go talk to Porter, or I'll go change the oil in my car. I can do all those things. Who says I need to only do one? I squeeze the sides of my head and fall against the wall, bumping the back of my skull on it.

Suddenly, slender arms wrap around me and hold me tight. I'm surprised. I open my eyes, through sweat and a racing heart, trying to fight the urge of the mania creeping in. They should know not to look at me like that, as if I'm expected to make a big speech. It fucks with me.

Mania is a form of bipolar disorder, and symptoms range for everyone. I have a lot of sleep deprivation, talking fast, excessive energy, violet urges, sexual urges, racing thoughts, and grandiosity.

For instance, I broke out of a mental institution. That is grandiosity.

I don't regret it for a minute.

"What are you doing, Goldie?" I ask, gasping for breath. She lays her cheek on my sweaty shirt and hugs me tighter.

"I read that hugs help lower your pulse and may help relieve stress. I never got to do it before. The institution wouldn't allow it," she states, somehow managing to hold me tighter. Her hands don't touch as they lay flat on my back.

I'm too shocked to reciprocate the hug for a minute, but then I realize, it's working. I wrap my arms around her and hold her tight. It's been so long since I've hugged someone, I forgot what it was like. They wouldn't let us touch each other in the institution. They were afraid we'd get too dangerous, so human contact is nice. It's going to be a habit I'm going to have to get used to.

Goldie is like a sister to me, so the fact that she went out of her way, out of her comfort zone, to care for me, won't be forgotten. She struggles a lot. I don't know much about her story, but the guards whispered. It was something about her husband dying that left her in the state she's in now.

She pushed her fears and sadness aside to help me, and for someone like her, that's an amazing sight to witness. "Thank you, Goldie. I feel better."

Her blonde hair tickles my nose as she leans back and peers up at me with permanent red eyes from crying. "Really?" the faintest of smiles appears on her lips. She hasn't smiled since I've known her.

"Really. Thank you." I kiss the top of her forehead and she steps back, but Oli slams against me next, knocking the breath out of me.

"Thank you," he says. "You saved us from that awful place."

I try to let go, to break the hug, but he shakes his head. "No, not yet. Three sets of three seconds."

"Of course, Oli." I hug him back too, and when he is ready to let go, he stops so abruptly. His hands drop and he takes a step back in a rush, but his left hand touches my side and then he slams against me again. "I'm sorry. One more time. I have to count perfectly. I can't touch you when I'm done."

"Whatever you need, Oli."

"Am I interrupting something?" Reaper stops at the screen door, then knocks.

"Just a second," Zipper hisses at my nephew. "Oli can't lose focus."

Reaper lifts up his hands in surrender. "I understand."

"Whatever. I'm sure you don't," Zipper bites. If there is someone who is close to functioning normally, it's Zipper. He looks worse than he is because of the scar on his mouth, but he has severe PTSD, and it isn't from being in the military. Something god awful happened to him, and it's left him unpredictable like the rest of us, but at least a normal conversation can flow with him.

"You'd be surprised how familiar I am with your situation," Reaper says just as Oli lets go, successfully not touching me.

He lets out a relieved breath and Felix comes up from behind Oli, sidesteps him, then gives me a hug too. "He's right," he says, giving me a quick pat on the back, then breaks the hug. "Duck!" he screams, and I drop to the ground along with everyone else when he whacks the air. He grins, "Okay, I got it. Pesky little demon butterfly. They have really sharp teeth."

Oh boy.

I'm so in over my head.

"I'm not giving you a hug," Zipper grimaces.

He doesn't like to be touched.

I push off the wall and nod to him in understanding. I don't need to say anything. I just need to let him know I understand. I turn toward the front door, which is hanging off the hinges. The only thing that locks is the screen door by a small piece of metal that can break with an easy tug.

Yep. I'm in so over my head that I'm pretty sure Porter buried me and all I see is fucking dirt. "Jesse—I mean, Reaper. Sorry. That will take getting used to. I've only known you as Jesse."

"It's okay," his deep voice grumbles, sounding similar to his father's. I won't tell him that. A beeping of a truck reversing has me looking over his shoulder, and I frown. "You going to let me in or are we going to talk through the screen all day?"

I jump out of my thoughts and scramble to open the screen door. "I'm sorry. I'm not used to having guests…" The old door creaks and when it opens, one of the damn hinges breaks and the bottom of the screen door bangs against the porch.

The rickety porch which groans in protest as Tool climbs the steps. He pauses, eyes the floor, then takes a step back. "I'm just going to stay right here," he points to the ground.

"Probably best. This place needs a lot of work," I say, suddenly embarrassed because I know how terrible we look, how the house looks, and I don't have anything to drink to offer him. "Reaper, can we go somewhere else to talk?"

Cigarette smoke lingers on Reaper, reminding me of the first time I caught his father smoking. Martin was behind the house, sitting next to a bush, and we were home alone. When he caught me, he wasn't mad, but he made me smoke with him.

I don't know how Reaper does it. It's the nastiest fucking habit ever.

"No, right here is fine. I haven't had a real chance to meet everyone. No one else came over for Christmas." Reaper lifts a brow at me, and I know that means he is asking me why no one else came.

"We aren't used to getting out," Zipper says. "We enjoy it here. It's fitting." Zipper doesn't say much but having Reaper here has triggered him. He sneers at the President of the Ruthless Kings, making the small dots—less than half inches apart on his top and bottom lip—slither and come alive in their own way.

"I understand," Reaper says, placing his hand on Zipper's shoulders.

Zipper jerks out of Reaper's hold. I can tell an episode is about to hit him. He looks around nervously, his eyes dashing back and forth between me and Goldie. "They are here! They are going to kill me. I can't take it anymore." He grips the side of his head and starts to cry. "They can't get me again. They can't."

"Zipper, everything is okay," I tell him, but he doesn't hear me. He is lost.

"No. Please. No more. I can't take it anymore," he pleads for his life, his cheeks wet from his tears.

Reaper steps forward to try and console him, but it's the worst thing he can do, because Zipper doesn't know him. Goldie rushes to his side and begins to cry, and Zipper presses his lips together, screaming as if they were stitching his mouth up all over again.

"Jesus Christ," Reaper says with regret. "I'm sorry. I… I didn't know. I should have been more careful."

"Goldie always calms him down." I explain. She does the one thing she always does; she tickles her hair over his nose.

She leans down and whispers in his ear, but I can't hear what she says. She presses her hand against his and it's a familiar touch that slowly brings him back. Post-traumatic stress disorder has a few tips to try and help someone out of an episode. It doesn't always work. Sight. Sound. Smell. Taste. Touch. Basically, anything consisting of the five senses has to be done to be brought back to the present.

I give them my back and stand in front of Reaper to give Goldie and Zipper some privacy. "Listen Reaper, my friends, they are delicate. There are things you don't know."

"And that would have been nice to fucking know before I came here. Let me get this straight, his trigger is touch, but touch bringing him out of an episode helps?"

"Only with someone he trusts, no offense."

"None taken," he says. He pinches his nose and lets out a breath. "You obviously do not have anyone here to help you all. You lied to me."

"I'm sorry. I was desperate. I'd do anything for them.

You don't know what it was like in the institution, Reaper. I was there all my life. It was awful."

He frowns, a look of guilt across his face. "If I would have known... I didn't... I'm sorry," he mumbles. "I really had no clue. I would have gotten you out. I don't give up on family. It's why I'm here. We obviously have a lot to talk about," he says, watching the scene over my shoulder. "We won't talk about it today. Is Porter still in his room?"

"Yes, safe and sound. And thank you, for sending food. I'm figuring it out," I say, sounding like a real low-life. I hate that I don't have my life together. I feel like I'm mooching off Reaper. I don't like that. I want to contribute. I want—as a man—to build my home into a safe place for me, for my friends, for the Kings if they ever for some reason to want to come over.

"I understand," Reaper chuckles. "Damn, I've said that so many times since walking through your doors."

"Reaper. Reaper. Reaper," Oli bounces over to us in his happy fashion. I don't know how he stays positive, but he's a bright light in the dark all of us seem to live in. "I'm Oli. Hi. Hi. Hi."

He holds out his hand and Reaper meets the shake with his palm, grinning. "Well, Hello, Oli. It's nice to meet you." Reaper tries to let go and Oli grips his hand harder, but Reaper doesn't see it as a challenge, so I let out a breath I didn't realize I was holding

"Three more seconds, please," Oli states.

"I'm in no rush, Oli." Reaper shows his patience and stands still, letting Oli work through his quirk.

Oli lets go and sighs. "Okay, there."

"You have a flying spider on your shoulder," Felix says, pointing to Reaper's shoulder with a shaky finger. Out of all of us, Felix is the one I worry about most. His schizophrenia is severe. He is always having delusions or hallucinations of some sort, even with medication. His meds make the delusions less severe.

"Here," Reaper says, catching on quick.

"Yeah. Right there," Felix gasps with wide, terrified eyes. "Be careful. It has spikes. Oh, I can't watch." He covers his eyes, and I chuckle, then clear my throat so I don't offend him.

"I need your help…" Reaper lets the sentence hang because he doesn't know Felix's name.

"Felix," I whisper in Reaper's ear.

"Felix, how will I know if I get him? I need you to tell me what to do." Reaper hovers his hand over his shoulder. There's nothing there, but Felix believes it and that's what matters.

Felix lowers his hand and gulps. "Okay. I'll help."

"Thank you," Reaper says, then slowly moves his hand. "Like this?"

"You have to be quick. It has wings."

Reaper slaps his hand down and grunts. Felix yells in fear and Reaper starts pretending to be in a raging battle with a fake flying spider. "Oh, wow! It's strong. Get something, Felix." Reaper struggles and slams his back against the wall.

Felix runs around the room and picks up a piece of

drywall that's fallen. He sprints to Reaper and lifts the weapon. "Like this?"

"Perfect. Now, when I let it go, you're going to smash it. It's the last of its kind, so we won't be seeing it anymore."

I have never used that tactic before. Everyone always says what he sees isn't real, but it's real to Felix. He doesn't need to hear they aren't real. He knows. He's scared of what he sees.

"Okay," Felix licks his lips, then wipes his left cheek on his shirt sleeve. "Ready."

"I'm counting on you," Reaper tells him. "You can't miss."

"I won't. I got it," Felix says, watching Reaper's hand like a hawk.

"On the count of three," Reaper says. "One. Two. Three." Reaper lets go and Felix watches something invisible fly in the air. He swings at it, then shouts in victory when it connects with the spider.

He smacks the floor with the drywall, and it cracks in half. "I think I got it," he says, dropping the weapon to the ground. Dust flies in the air, and it looks like a cloud of smoke swirling around Felix. "I did it," he smiles

"High-five, man." Reaper holds up his hand and Felix slaps his palm eagerly.

"Hey? We gonna fuck around all day or are we going to clean this place up and unload the truck?" Tool interrupts. He takes the screwdriver behind his ear and fixes the hinge the screen door is attached to. He tries to open it and it glides smoothly. "This won't last much longer. Good thing we got a new one, which, I guess I shouldn't have fixed it. I couldn't help myself."

"Truck? What's he talking about, Reaper?" I ask him.

"We got some furniture for you, and we want to help get the priority rooms fixed, like the bathrooms and bedrooms. It won't be an overnight job, but it's a project I want to work on with you and your friends," Reaper says. "If that's okay."

I'm stunned. I'm left speechless and I get a bit choked up. No one has ever done anything like this for us. No one has ever cared enough. "I… why?" I stumble over my words.

"You're family, Uncle Zain. I won't lose more time," he says. "We're going to fix the roof first. Okay? It's why we are here so early." Reaper walks outside as if he didn't flip my world upside down.

Family.

The one thing I never thought I'd have.

I have a family.

CHAPTER TWO

Zain

IT TOOK THREE DAYS FROM SUNRISE TO SUNSET TO GET THE ROOF on. Half of the club worked inside, cleaning it up, fixing the walls, and updating the kitchen. The asylum rooms, even Porter's, are cleaned and updated. The men have worked around the clock for more than two weeks now. It isn't perfect, but it's livable. Some areas have remained the same, like the main hallway. The ceiling is fixed, but the floor is original concrete. The walls are cracked, but Reaper put this plastic protective barrier over it to give us some stability. The wheelchairs are sitting where we found them, awkwardly placed along the wall.

I don't think they look as creepy as when someone is in them, mind numb with medication and nearly catatonic. I'd rather see an empty chair, than an occupied one. Nothing will haunt me more than remembering the vacant stare of a patient in a wheelchair. They look directly through you. It's unsettling to say the least.

Imagine your blood running cold and the air being sucked out of the room. You're shivering. A tingle drifts down your spine, and you feel frozen in place, unable to move your feet from the glare. For a brief moment, a trembling second, you're a statue.

And then they get wheeled away and you can breathe again and feel the warmth in your body.

It's fitting to leave parts of the asylum original.

Crazy deserves to be appreciated. When you know the horrible things that happened here.

There are even a few padded rooms downstairs, used straitjackets collecting dust in a closet, and mouth guards to keep patients from biting their tongues off through electro-shock therapy.

Reaper asked if I wanted to get rid of them. I should have said yes, but something held me back. What if one of us needs a padded room? So I said no.

It's the next room on the list to get an overhaul.

I sit down on the new porch steps and crack a beer open, then lean my head against the beam. It's late. Everyone has worked their asses off and most of everyone is inside asleep. The majority of the asylum rooms have been turned into bedrooms. A few of Reaper's men are staying here until all the work is done.

"How are your tattoos doing? Two nights of pure pain by Luci and Bobby Jane couldn't have been easy," Reaper chuckles, taking a seat next to me on the steps.

He's paid Luci and Bobby-Jane extra to come to the Asylum after hours to tattoo me a few weeks back. Anything I wanted. When I told Reaper I liked his tattoos, he asked if I wanted them.

I did, but someone can't get tattooed in a mental institution.

And with a snap of a finger, Reaper made my wish happen. I could have left my friends here with people they didn't know, but I wasn't comfortable with that. They needed me here in case anything happened.

Ironically, the guy they call Luci, full name Lucifer, tattooed the devil on my arm. He's talented, which makes sense that he would own his own tattoo shop.

"Good. I'm ready for more," I say with a laugh.

"That's what always happens."

I clink our beer bottles together and take a drink of the citrus flavored amber.

"Should you be drinking that with your…" Reaper tries to find the words as he hums. "Because of, you know," he says, then silences himself with a swallow of beer.

"My medication?"

"Yeah, I'm sorry. I shouldn't ask, but I need to know. You guys don't live far. Sarah is pregnant, and I honestly don't know any of you. I need to make sure my club is safe."

"I understand. When a nurse gets here, I'll talk to her. I can't take the stuff from the institution. It made me a zombie."

"I feel fucking terrible my dad left you in there. He wasn't the best man, but I never thought he'd do that."

"No one understood what was wrong with me growing up. I got in a lot of school fights. Constantly breaking shit. Attacked teachers. Attacked other kids. One day I nearly burned down the school. And then I genuinely would not remember anything when I'd come out of my manic state, and I'd look around and everyone else was horrified. I think he only did what he knew to do. I don't fault him, but I do fault him for not trying harder for me."

"Yeah, he had a habit of doing that. You met Delilah, right? The sister I knew nothing about. I bet he knew. That fucking bastard." Reaper takes an irate swig of beer, a snarl lingering on his breath when the bottle pops from his lips as he stares into the desert night. "I just… I know this is unusual. This place. This asylum. I know you have your issues, but you're family. Blood. You and your friends have the protection of the club."

"I appreciate that," I say, doing my best not to sound too excited. "You didn't have to go and do all this. The beds, the furniture, the repairs, it'll be awhile before I can pay you back." I scratch the back of my head, wondering if and when I'll be able to pay him back. "Maybe a payment plan? I need to find a job, under the books. I can't find a regular job. No one will want to hire me. I just need some time—"

"—No time. There is nothing to pay back. Okay? You're family. I'm helping you, and as far as I'm concerned you worked your ass off for the last thirty years. You deserve this. You're just getting what's owed to you. And I can get you a job. Consider yourself a bartender at Kings' Club. You okay with that? Or you want to be in the back? Like the kitchen?"

LUNATIC

My beer falls from my hand, spilling on my boot, and the bottle thuds down the steps. The glass rolls few inches across the sand, the beer leaving a wet trail. "You're serious? You'd do that?" My thoughts start racing about the opportunity. Maybe one day I'll be able to get my own place, run it, be the owner. I could do it. I bend my head forward and place it between my knees and take deep breaths. If I don't calm down, I'm going to do something stupid, like try to go and buy a club and try to run it.

"Hey—" Reaper wraps an arm around my shoulder. "Of course, I'd do it. You're my Uncle. This is the least I can do."

"You have no idea how much this means to me," I tell him. Emotion overflows in me, but it's not my mania. It's a new feeling. A feeling of gratitude. I welcome the sense of being wanted. It sounds ridiculous, but all my life I've been alone, especially when I was in the institution. Isolation is the worst and accepting help and love will be new to me. "Thank you."

Reaper brushes me off as if it's nothing. "I mean it, man. And if it doesn't work out at Kings' Club, we'll find you something else. But I know you can step up to the plate. You're a hell of a man, taking care of your friends like this. I respect the hell out of that."

I look at him, wetness brimming in my eyes. I don't even know what to say.

"Well—" Reaper drains his beer and stands. "I gotta get going. Sarah's waiting for me."

"How is she doing? Is she doing okay?"

"So far, so good. She's beautiful. Her stomach is starting to swell. Barely, but I notice, and I can't seem to ever pull my hand away. We've been trying for a long time. She miscarried awhile back. Trying to get pregnant has been a long, exhausting road."

"I'm happy for you. I hope—" I take a long deep breath, because I don't know if I'm allowed to say this, but I need a few extra seconds, "—I hope I'll be able to meet him, and/or her."

He gives me a look of disbelief, brows raised, and then he tosses his head back and laughs.

A stab of disappointment hits me in the heart, and I chortle. Of course he doesn't want me around his family. I'm too unstable. I snag another beer out of the cooler and twist off the top. I shouldn't be so upset. He's just met me. He doesn't remember me from when he was a baby. This relationship is going to be a long road. I'm willing to put in the travel, the time, and hopefully he and I can get to a place where he can trust me.

"Are you kidding? I'm not going to have my kid miss out on time with his Great Uncle. You better be ready for that title." Reaper gives a parting goodbye grip, squeezing my shoulder before he pulls out a cigarette. "Relax, Uncle Zain. You're home now."

He opens up the driver's side door of the midnight black Ford Raptor. He steps up on the foot rail and before he dips his head down, he leans one elbow on top of the truck and the other on the door. "I'll see you bright and early, Uncle Zain."

LUNATIC

"Yeah, bright and early," I choke out, holding in the emotion as I raise my beer in the air as he leaves. He waves goodbye and starts the truck. The horsepower grumbling the air is almost as impressive as a Harley's. The tires roll back as he leaves, crunching against dead bushes and rocks. The headlights blind me for a second and I turn away, blinking toward the sky. The floating circular rings take over my vision for a second and Reaper gives one last honk before vanishing into the dark.

It's just me out here now. Everyone else is asleep. I inhale the air, letting the smells of the earth and the hint of cold drape over my lungs. The world smells so good after breathing the same damn air in the mental institution. I swear there was something in it that helped make the crazy stay and linger in you.

I lean back on my elbows and stare up at the sky. The stars twinkle and blink, and the endless abyss is a blanket of black, with slight hues of dark blue. The open space that allows me to see the countless constellations has me a little more mesmerized than I ought to be. It's been a long time since I've been able to see something that hasn't been blocked by bars on the outside of a window.

I'll never take anything beautiful for granted.

"It's such a gorgeous night!" a sweet, harmonic voice says from out of nowhere.

I sit up and glance around, staring back and forth to see if I can spot who the voice belongs to. I don't see a damn thing. "Shit, maybe Reaper is right. I don't need to be drinking right now." I set the beer down and rub my eyes, fucking exhausted. It's hard to sleep when my mind is always on, constantly with the thoughts, and battling the urge to not fucking lose it.

A giggle from my left wakes me up. I stand and run down the steps, wondering where the hell it is coming from.

"So much space!" The angelic tone is a song filtering through the exhaustion.

She's getting closer now. It's cold out here, and dark. What if she's lost? She'll need help. I spin around again, staring over the outline of the cactuses, but then the scuff and grind of sand sounds from behind me. I turn, holding my breath when the faint glow of the porch light illuminates against platinum blonde hair. Her arms are above her head, and she's smiling as if she isn't in forty-degree weather wearing a black dress that blends in with the night. Her skin is the color of cream, the kind someone puts in their coffee.

I'm enamored.

I stand there, staring at the most beautiful creature I've ever seen, watching her spin and dip like she's a ballerina. Her movements are smooth and effortless, like waves in the sea, flowing in constant sets of perfection. One arm reaches out, like she's stretching to touch an object that has her attention, and damn it, I wish it was me. Her back leg lifts and her dress dips low in the back and the material in the front falls over the leg on the ground.

My thoughts start to race, imagining her in my arms in bed, kissing her plump lips that are red from the cold air of the night, grabbing her tits that bounce with every graceful move she makes, and wanting her to be mine.

Only mine.

It's dangerous when a man like me wants so deeply because I don't have the ability to let go.

And I know if she were to ever be mine, I wouldn't allow her to let go.

I'd take her will.

I'd take her freedom.

I'd take.

Until all there was in her world was me. All she could ever want is me.

She spins again, her feet bare and dirty. Her dress is, too. It's a bit torn along the edges as if she's been out here for too long. She laughs again, a sound that has my cock turning to stone. Her eyes are closed, dancing as if she's been twirling across the desert for days. When she tilts her head back, face up toward the sky, another smile plays along her lips as if she's experiencing euphoria with every move. The golden blonde locks cascade down her back, almost touching the ground as she bends backward.

Fucking hell, she's a masterpiece.

Her breasts press against the tight material of her dress, her cleavage teasing the control of my tongue has it flicks inside my mouth.

Her leg lifts again before she quickly presses her foot to the ground.

I'm hypnotized.

Where the hell did she come from? Why is she here?

Does she realize the mistake she's made by me seeing her?

Her left hand drags up her right arm, grazing the smooth flesh, until her fingers dip between her breasts, then skim over the curve of her neck where I want to press my lips. The half moon is bright since there are no clouds in the sky, and it shines against the sweat on her neck. She is glistening. She's a ballerina dipped in glitter and she's too glamorous for the likes of me.

I don't care.

I'm too caught up in the movement of her body and the ache in my cock to notice she's getting too close to the bikes. One last twirl and she smacks against one with her hip. She gasps, finally opening her eyes, but it is too late.

The bike rocks, and for a moment I don't think it's going to fall.

She's reaches to stop it, but it's too late.

The bike crashes to the ground, the mirror snapping off when it hits, the glass shattering into pieces.

Oh, Tool is going to be pissed.

I snap out of the trance I'm in and hurry over to her. "Are you okay?"

When she hears me, she's startled, because she hasn't seen me this entire time. She looks from me, to the asylum, then back to me.

I bend down to pick up the bike and set it up right, making a note to take blame for the mirror.

When she doesn't answer me, I start to get concerned. "Hey, what's your name?" I brush my thumb over her cheek and rub the dirt off, but the moment I touch her skin, the edges of my vision blur when I feel how delicate she is.

LUNATIC

Oh, she's made a mistake coming here, because I'm never going to allow her to leave.

"Chloe," she says softly, her big hazel eyes locking with mine.

Chloe.

I love her already.

CHAPTER THREE

Chloe

How did I get here? I can't remember.
Oh no.
I think I might have blacked out again.

I take in my surroundings, seeing nothing but the vast desert and feeling the vow of winter drifting over my skin. I take in a shuttering breath and rub my hands up and down my arms. I realize I've been quiet for far too long and tilt my head back to stare at the man's face. When I see him, I take a step away, feeling small as he stares at me.

His eyes are brown with flecks of garnet, and the left side of his face is lit by the light casting down the porch. He has a smooth head and a brown, thick beard. From shoulder to shoulder, he must be three of me side by side. It's obvious he is in great shape, perfect for a lumberjack.

LUNATIC

He's beautiful, but something dark hides behind those demented eyes—and like a twist of unpredictable fate, I'm caught in the reflection of the stars swirling in pools of endless ink.

"You're cold," he states, unbuttoning his flannel shirt to expose his chest.

"Um." I glance away, my cheeks turning a hot shade of pink. I'm thankful he can't see me. His chest is hairy, and his nipples are tight buds of pink from the chill in the air. As he pulls his arms out of the sleeves, my cold quivering body suddenly heats when I see his skin decorated in tattoos. It's too dark to tell them apart.

Well.

All but one.

There's a devil on his forearm, colored in red and wearing a black top hat. He throws the flannel over my shoulders, and I sigh in relief. The material is still warm from his body, and I can smell the workday sticking to his shirt. I lift the flannel to my nose and inhale, loving the wild spice marinating the flannel.

"I'm Zain," he growls, squeezing his eyes shut, then shaking his head. His fists clench at his sides and that's when I notice roman numerals tattooed on him. His tattoos are fresh, like he just got them done in the last few weeks.

Wow.

That's a lot of work to get done all at once.

"I like your tattoos," I say, wrapping the lapels of the shirt around me tighter as the breeze blows and pebbles the skin along my chest.

"Thank you. They are yours," he states, placing a hand on my lower back.

I don't understand what he means. They are mine? Maybe he didn't mean to say that.

"Let's get you inside. It's cold."

We walk toward the large house that has a new wrap around porch and steps. There's a sign to the right of the steps, much older than the rails leading up the staircase.

The Asylum.

My heart pounds against my chest, my ribcage trembling from the force as I read the words. Is this an insane house? No. Maybe it's a joke between friends. It has to be.

Zain opens the screen door. I notice it's aged, too, the white paint chipped and faded, showing rotten wood. The screen itself is torn, only hanging on by rusted staples, but the front door is new. It's painted black, an unwelcoming color. He turns the silver knob to open the door.

"I'm sorry it's a mess. We're renovating the place," he explains.

I step in front of him, and my dirty feet leave dust on the new hardwood floors. I shuffle my feet, only making the mess worse, and jump backward until I'm outside. "I'm a mess. I don't want to ruin your house."

"Are you kidding? This place is messy as is, but if you want, I'll carry you to the restroom where you can clean up. I can bring you some clothes."

I want to ask for one of his flannels to wrap myself in so I can sleep comfortable tonight. While I'm lying in bed or on the couch, wherever he decides to put me, I want him to talk to me in his whiskey-ridden voice. Every time he speaks, my body burns to the graveled depths, and to drunkenly fall asleep listening to him sounds like it would give me sweet dreams.

"Okay," I say quietly.

I haven't said much, and he hasn't asked much.

I hope he doesn't.

Truth is, I really don't know how I got here. All I remember is the loud crash and then staring down at a motorcycle.

I know who I am and where I'm from, and there is only one way that I got here. My thoughts are interrupted when Zain swings me into the air and crosses the threshold. Something about the gesture seems primal as he holds me tight to his body.

Tighter than he should.

But I like it.

Not that I'd ever tell him.

I don't know him well enough to say that.

Zain kicks the door shut, and there's no one in the living room. The house is eerily quiet.

"Everyone is sleeping. It's been an exhausting few days trying to get this house up to code. You'll meet everyone in the morning."

"And then I can call my dad and tell him to come get me?" I ask.

He doesn't answer me, not really. He grunts and holds me closer, taking me through the open space of the living room and kitchen. There's a large red U-shaped sectional and flat screen TV mounted to the wall. Other than that, everything else seems bare. There are no chairs, no artwork or rugs, and there are plastic sheets hanging from certain walls.

We take a left and start heading down a hallway that has cracked walls and flickering lights. I clutch onto Zain because that's all I have to hold onto, then hold my breath when I see a rusted wheelchair against the wall.

What if this place really is an asylum?

"Where are you taking me?" I ask in a small, frightened voice. There isn't a noise to be heard. It's just his footsteps down the long corridor.

"My room," he answers simply.

"Put me down." The threat of tears burns; I wiggle in his hold, but he holds tight. "Please. You're scaring me. Please," I beg, a hot droplet falling against my cheek.

"I'd never hurt you." He flips me around like I weigh nothing, and my legs part naturally to wrap around his hips. He seems genuine and sad that I'd be afraid of him. "Ever. I only want to keep you safe." The intensity of his eyes lightens, and a few lines pinch on either side of his eyes, showing crow's feet. He's older than me, by at least fifteen years.

He's so handsome, but something about him has the hairs on my arms standing up as if there is too much static electricity in the room.

I can't decipher if that's a good thing or a bad thing.

"You don't even know me. I don't know you. This is inappropriate," I say, swallowing as his big palm rests against my cheek.

LUNATIC

There it is again—the static. I can't decide if his touch promises good or evil.

"I want to know everything about you, Chloe."

I jostle against his body when he begins to walk again. "Why?" I ask. No one ever wants to get to know me. I'm too much for them to handle. That's what everyone tells me, anyway. My parents locked me away, and my therapist was the only one that ever gave me the time of day.

I liked Dr. Washington. Too much.

"It's one of the things I know I have to do," he says. "I *have* to." He opens his bedroom door, and I stare over his shoulder to see the dark tunnel of hallway, the wheelchairs giving me a taste of discomfort. "You don't understand how much I need to," he raises his voice, and I flinch away since his mouth his right next to my ear.

Zain places me on his bed, right on the edge, and unwraps his arms from me, and my fingertips run across his chest as I lower my arms.

Static again.

He growls from the contact, brushing his lips across my cheek. "You are everything my wildest dreams could have ever imagined."

I swallow the lump in my throat, unable to move, unable to breathe. He inhales, dragging his nose across my jawline. "You smell amazing," he says, gathering the thick of my hair and dragging it behind my shoulder. "I'll go fill the tub for you. It's new, never used. I hope you like it. I'll even add bubbles. You like bubbles, right? I hear all women like bubble baths. I have salts too. You want salts?" He is talking so fast I can hardy understand him. "I'll add them all for you. Anything you want. I'll make sure you have it all."

I'm too shocked to say anything, so I just blink.

He runs a hand over his bald head and grins at me. "You'll like it. I promise." He presses a kiss on my neck, right as my pulse jumps, and I close my eyes, wanting to feel his lips again. "You'll be taken care of. I'll make sure of that."

Zain backs away from me, pulling the energy being created between us tight. He turns and walks toward the bathroom, his wide back flexing, showing his ropes of muscle. I look away, tucking a piece of blonde hair behind my ear, blushing like the virgin that I am. I've been around men before, but I've never been around someone like Zain.

He's intense, and that's putting it lightly.

He scares me, intrigues me, and turns me on all at the same time.

A complete stranger. What in the world have I come to?

The bath water turns on and the masculine hum of Zain's singing has a faint smile playing on my lips. His voice is low, reminding me of a trombone a deep note vibrating the air. While he is preparing the bathtub, I take the time to study the bedroom. The walls have a fresh paint of light grey, and the lights that hang down around the room are simple, yet charming in a rustic way. The bulb is inside a mason jar and the wire is a copper color attached to the ceiling. The bed is big, with a soft mattress and a forest green comforter. It's very masculine, which fits Zain perfectly. There is another set of doors to the right of the bathroom, big wooden pieces that slide open. I wonder if that's the closest.

Or maybe his torture chamber.

No. I'm getting myself all worked up for no reason. He seems nice. He welcomed me into his home. And there are other people here too, so he can't be too bad. Right?

"Your bath is ready," he informs me, his voice coming closer as he walks into the bedroom. He holds out his hand for me to take, and I lay my fingers across his, hoping I'm not making a terrible mistake by trusting him.

He leads me to the bathroom, my feet leaving dirty imprints across his new floor again. I sigh, thinking about how I got here. I hate it when I black out. It always leaves me with more questions.

"Do you like it?" Zain asks, laying his hands on my shoulders as I stare at the bubble bath. He lit candles too, and the lavender aroma carries with the steam coming from the tub. "I wanted you to relax. When you're ready we can talk about what had you dancing in the middle of the desert at night."

I chuckle and stare at him in confusion, titling my head. "Zain, I don't dance. What are you talking about?"

"That's impossible, Chloe. I saw you. I watched you. You danced, and it was beautiful, right before you crashed into one of the motorcycles."

"Well, that's impossible. Like I said, I don't know how to dance." I bend down to test the water. It's hot, just the way I like it.

"Chloe, are you okay?" he asks. So kind and considerate.

I turn to look over my shoulder and smirk. "Chloe isn't here right now," I say to my rescuer. "But we haven't had a chance to meet." I stand, looking the big man up and down. Damn, he is a bear. I run my fingers through his chest hair and moan, biting my lip when I feel the muscles tense under my touch.

I lift my other hand and untie the halter top of my dress. It falls to the ground and the man in front of me looks his fill, staring at my breasts.

"I'm Jessica. And who are you, handsome?"

CHAPTER FOUR

Zain

I KNEW SHE WAS BEAUTIFUL, BUT HER BODY EXCEEDED MY expectations. Her tits are round and perky, with tight pink buds. Her waist dips and flares out to her curvy hips and thick thighs. She has her belly button pierced, something I didn't expect from Chloe.

But maybe it wasn't Chloe's idea.

I would ask if she's kidding or pulling my leg, but I've been around enough mental patients to know when someone has a split personality disorder.

Chloe would have never dropped her dress in front of me. She seemed too bashful, but Jessica seems to be her polar opposite.

Her hand drops to my hard cock, and I grunt when she squeezes. "Such a big man," she purrs, tossing her hair over her shoulder. "What's your name?" she asks again, taking her hand away and turning around to get into the tub.

My eyes follow the smooth length of her spine to her peach-shaped ass as she takes the step in order to get into the tub.

"Zain," I say, my tone deep and husky as I watch her sink into the water and the bubbles.

She's trouble.

The kind of trouble I can't have around here if I want to make a life for myself.

I'm not surprised to know she has another personality. Maybe I should be, but I've been conditioned to appreciate insanity, or she might have run me off.

The prettiest ones are always the craziest.

Damn, looks like I'm asking for trouble, then.

"Zain," she tests my name out on her tongue, then giggles, swishing the bubbles around until her breasts are completely covered. The water glistens over the curve of her tits. Her golden mane is wet, decorated with white foam. She lifts her leg in the air, showing me how flexible she is. "I hear you like how I dance. Why don't you join me, and we can talk about it?" she teases, slowly lowering her leg back into the water.

A good man would refuse, turn his back, and walk away.

I unbutton my pants and watch her face, her eyes dropping to where I grab the zipper.

A man with mania is not a good man, especially when he has a new obsession. She's never going to be able to leave.

I'm too... manic with the need to make her mine. I'll lock her in one of those padded rooms if I have to.

And if Jessica even thinks about hurting my people, I'll put her in a straitjacket and wait for Chloe to come back. Sounds fun.

"I didn't think you'd take me up on the offer," she says.

"Well, I don't think Chloe would appreciate this, but it's a good thing I'm not talking to Chloe, isn't it?" I kick off my jeans, and my cock bounces when it's released from the uncomfortable denim. I wrap my hand around myself and give myself a few pumps, holding back a groan as I stare at her.

"Chloe would blush. She's a virgin. She wouldn't be able to handle you," Jessica purrs, her breath speeding up as she watches a dollop of precome leave my slit. I wipe it off with my thumb and press it against my mouth.

She wants to test me with her rebellion. Fine.

I'll test her too.

I lift my leg and step into the tub, the hot water melting the cold night away. I sit on the other edge, keeping my space from Jessica, my cock still impossibly hard in the high heat of the tub.

"Are you a virgin?" I ask her, reaching for the stainless-steel door of the minifridge Reaper insisted I install into wall. I thought it was pointless, but what do you know? First night and it is already in use. "Drink?"

"Yes, please," she says.

I twist the top off a beer and hand it to her, then open another for myself. "So, are you a virgin?"

"No." She winks. "We would have no fun if I left it up to her." She brings the bottle to her lips and takes a swallow. I'm entranced at the way her throat muscles move as the liquid rushes to her belly.

It isn't often that another personality is aware of one, but it happens. Jessica must know of Chloe, but I wonder if Chloe knows of Jessica. Chloe seems to be her original personality, which is usually meeker than the alter. Jessica seems feisty, like someone who would like to bring havoc on the world. But then there is Chloe.

Sweet, gentle, and shy.

Both are everything I could want.

Which is good, because Jessica would be the one to handle the manic side of me I think, while Chloe would get the other side.

I might not have another personality, but I have two sides of me, and both want this one woman.

"You're staring," she says, taking another sip.

"You're impossible not to stare at, Jessica."

"Why aren't you surprised?" she asks, setting her beer on the edge of the tub. She leans forward, her hair spreading around the water like lily pads, and she lays her hands on my shins. Her touch has me closing my eyes, knowing damn good and well this shouldn't be happening with someone I just met.

But something is different about her. Something that makes me want to move fast. I'm already thinking about whisking her away and getting married. I could blame it on grandiosity, but the more I think about it, the more I want to do it.

Maybe tomorrow. I'll take her somewhere in Vegas. She'll be mine. All mine. Yes. I have to do it.

Then she can never leave me.

They can never leave me.

"So many people freak out when they find out I'm a part of Chloe, yet you don't bat an eye. Why?" she asks, tilting her head as she digs her nails into my thigh.

"I'm experienced in this kind of thing, you could say."

"Oh, you're going to have to give me more than that," she says, sliding her hands closer to my cock.

"You're in an asylum, sweet girl." I lift my hand and press two fingers under her chin. "Put two and two together."

"You mean, we've wandered into an actual mental institution?" Her eyes light up and her voice raises on the verge of excitement.

"What used to be, yes. Everyone that lives here escaped from one recently."

"Oh, do tell that story. What is your—" she wraps her hand around my cock and squeezes "—vice?"

I gasp, clenching my teeth together and loving her strokes of confidence. Chloe wouldn't dare, and that's what has me reaching down and wrapping my fingers around her wrist, pulling her hand off me. I must be fucking stupid for denying her touch. Just like Chloe, I'm a virgin too. Being locked up in a mental institution doesn't give a man many opportunities to roam around and have sex.

I tried sneaking away with a patient or two, but I always got caught, tased, then thrown back in my room. Yeah, it isn't like I announce that I've never had sex. I'm a grown fucking man, but I'm not about to do it now. Circumstance is everything, and I haven't been in the time or place to give in to my desires.

And even if the place is giving me a chance now, it isn't the time.

I won't have sex with Jessica until Chloe is on board. I wouldn't feel right about it, no matter how badly I want to taste her.

"A story for a story, sweet girl," I reply, trying to get my raging libido under control.

She snarls at me and uses my legs to push away to the other side of the tub. "I am not a sweet girl," she says, bringing her knees to her chest. A delicate position for a woman so confident.

"What brought you to the middle of the desert?" I probe, wanting to know the truth. How did a woman like her get away? Doesn't someone miss her? Doesn't someone love her?

I'd miss her.

She's too magnetic for me to ever forget.

And if she ever tried to dance away from me, she wouldn't get far. I'd stop her mid-twirl and swing her back to into my arms.

Then lock her in that padded room where she can never escape.

I'm serious when I say that my obsession for things I want is intense. The way I want her, the way my body burns, the way my mind spins to get lost in the deception of my illness for her, is a catastrophe.

And I want to be in the middle of it, feeling the destruction of the world as her and I come together.

I don't know how to handle her just yet. Jessica seems unpredictable, and Chloe is a wallflower that doesn't like attention. I'd have to handle each side of her with a different touch. I'm up for the challenge, and I know if Jessica heard my truth, she'd want to come at me full force.

I need to gain the trust of her original personality. Spill my secrets to her and hope she can accept them. And if she can't?

Well, too damn bad.

One day she will, then eventually she'll learn to love me.

Thinking back, the only thing I've ever been so obsessed about was escaping the mental prison and abuse over the last thirty-five years.

My entire life.

I don't know what the world is like or what it has to offer, but I think for some reason, Chloe and Jessica arriving at my doorstep was no coincidence. She's here to make my transition to the real world better. To make my world… meaningful.

As I'm looking at Jessica's defiant expression—chin up, jaw clenched, with lust in her eyes as she stares at me, I know exactly the kind of woman I've been wanting and haven't had a chance to have. I know as boys grow into men, they like blondes or brunettes, redheads, or raven-colored hair. Big chest? Small? Ass man? I never got to have these conversations, so I never knew. Sure, there were a few pretty women in and out of the institution, but the chance to be alone with them never happened, and none of them grabbed my attention enough.

My focus was on getting the hell out of a place that was killing me slowly.

I'm alive more than ever and I've figured out my type.

Fucking crazy blondes with two personalities.

It suits me, considering how I was raised.

"Are you going to tell me or sit there and stare at me all day, sweet girl?"

She smirks, chugging her beer down until it's empty, then sets the bottle aside. "That's for me to know." She glances away from me and then all of a sudden, her brows dip in the middle in confusion. Her blonde hair swishes back and forth along the fading bubbles. She looks lost.

"Jessica?"

She snaps her head up and her eyes widen, the flame from the candles dancing in the big pupils in the middle of her irises. She screams, covering her breasts with her hands, and tears fill her eyes. "What... what happened? Why are we in the tub? What did you do to me? Oh god," she cries, piercing my heart.

I hate to see her panic.

This is Chloe, I have no doubt.

Internally, I growl when I think about Jessica leaving me mid-conversation in the bathtub for Chloe to find herself in this position with me. Little hellion, just wait until she appears again.

"Chloe," I start softly, keeping my tone low and gentle

to try and ease her fear. "You're safe. I'm not going to hurt you. Do you remember anything about how you got here?"

A tear drips down her cheek and she shakes her head, staring at the exit of the bathroom. She keeps her hands covering her chest and the bubbles are still piled high all over her body, so the glorious shape is hidden. "It's fuzzy. I remember coming into the bathroom, and then darkness. Can we get out of the tub? I don't know you well enough to be in here with you. Please," she asks with a trembling voice.

"How about I leave? You're supposed to get cleaned up from being in the desert. I'm only in here because—"

"I know," she whispers, unable to look at me. "I know what happens when I black out. I know about Jessica. It took me years to understand what was happening to me. She seduced you into the tub. Did we… Did she—"

It takes me a minute to realize what she means. "No, we didn't have sex. I wouldn't do that, especially after what I just learned about you. I'm not that kind of man."

Well, I'm just realizing all sorts of things about myself tonight, aren't I? "She did…"

"What?" she snaps. "What did she do?"

"She grabbed my dick."

She buries her face in her hands and her shoulders shake. "I'm so sorry. She's always been so forward and—"

"Hey, I'm not perfect. I can't sit here and tell you I didn't like it, because I did, but I took her hand off me because I wasn't comfortable with you not knowing about it. This is a difficult situation, and I'm going to do my best by respecting your wishes and hers. And she didn't seduce me.

She challenged me. I'm not one to back down from a challenge, though."

"Yeah, she's good at that," she scoffs, her hand skimming over the bubbles, creating different shapes with the moldable foam.

"I'll go," I tell her, using the edge of the tub to push myself out of the tub.

Chloe watches me, her eyes so different from Jessica's. There's so much innocence in them. The two personalities are so different, and I love their differences. The water cascades down my body, my cock pointing straight to the ceiling, and bubbles create a ring around the base. I'm not ashamed for her to see how she affects me; I can't hide my reaction.

I won't apologize for it either.

She bites the side of her lip—something her and Jessica have in common—and bashfully looks away. There is a smile tugging at her lips, like maybe she's happy to see me like this, but I'm not going to jump to conclusions. I've only known her for a few hours.

I grab a towel off the hook and wrap it around my waist. "I'll leave you alone, Chloe. I'm sorry for interrupting your bath." I walk backward and grab the doorknob as I go. "I'll go get you some clothes, okay? If you get done before I get back, then there is a robe in the closet." I point to the double doors next to the tub. My feet make a squishing sound against the black tile floor since they are wet, but at least they are warm.

Reaper wanted me to have the best, so he installed

heated floors and towel warmers. I didn't know things like that existed until he had them delivered. He took care of everything. He gathered my clothes and shoe sizes, then everyone else's and had Sarah and the rest of the ol' ladies go shopping for everyone.

I never would have asked for candles and bubble bath but now I'm incredibly happy she put them in my bathroom closet. I have everything I've ever wanted and more.

Almost.

I somehow need to figure out how to make two women who encompass the same mind fall in love with me.

"Thank you," she says, finally bringing her eyes to me. They linger on my chest, then down my arms, and she blushes again.

I close the door and sigh. She probably wants the door locked, but the problem with that is, I don't believe in locks. The only rooms in this house that can lock are the padded rooms, Porter's room, and the front door. I've been locked away for far too long, and now that I have my freedom, there is no way in hell I'm going to trap myself.

I feel an itch on my arm and scratch it, then look down at my devil tattoo.

Fuck.

Luci said I wasn't allowed to scratch them once I took the bandage off, no matter how bad it itches. And it itches like hell right now. I run to the mirror hanging on wall beside the bed and study my arms, flexing and turning them every way I can to make sure all of them are okay. I've been washing them and applying lotion like he instructed. I quickly toss a bit of soap and water on the devil to rehydrate the skin, rubbing my hand softly over it, then shuck the towel off and pat the devil dry, sighing when I see it's okay.

I hope it stays that way.

Sliding open the closet door, I grab a pair of new flannel pajamas, step into them, and tie them tighter around my hips. I give the bathroom door one last look knowing the woman of my dreams is naked behind it, but she's trusting me to take care of her.

Chloe is, anyway. Jessica seems to be an 'I can take care of myself' kind of woman.

Which is both hot and infuriating.

I make my way out of the bedroom and down the hall until I get to Goldie's room. I knock, and it doesn't take long for her to answer. When she does, she has fresh tears on her cheeks, and the first thing I do is engulf her in a hug.

"I'm okay," she sniffles.

She's spoken to us so much more since we have left the institution. I hope she's on a journey where she's finding herself again. Goldie deserves the best. "You sure?"

She nods, wiping her cheeks. "What can I help you with, Zain?"

"Do you have a pair of pajamas and underwear?"

She looks me up and down and shakes her head. "Sorry, Zain. They won't fit you."

I snort and chuckle. "Not for me. There is a woman here who was lost and found her way here to the asylum somehow. I just want to make sure she's comfortable."

"Another woman in the house?" she gets excited, and I

don't have the heart to tell her she might not be able to be friends with one of them.

Jessica doesn't scream pillow talk and painted nails. More like scratch your face and kick you in the balls.

"Wait here." She turns around, and I hear a few drawers open and close. "Here," she says, opening the door a bit wider, and that's when I see Zipper lying in her bed sleeping.

"Is he okay?"

"Yeah, sleeping off the exhaustion is all, from the episode. When can I meet her?" she asks excitedly, tears dried.

"I don't know. She's pretty shaken up. Thank you for these, Goldie. If you ever need anything, let me know." I lean in and kiss her forehead and wonder why Goldie and I never stood a chance. She's gorgeous with her dirty blonde hair and puppy dog eyes, but I want to protect her like my little sister, if I had one. The lust, the attraction, it was never there.

Not like how it is with Chloe and Jessica.

Fuck me, I feel like I hit the lottery. A two in one.

"I will. Have a goodnight," she says.

"Night, Goldie." I hurry down the haunted hall toward my room and open the door. "Chloe? I have your—" I pause when I see her in the bed. She's wearing the oversized robe and is tucked under the covers, asleep. Shutting the door, I press against it and smile.

She's obviously comfortable enough to sleep here without her walls up.

I just need to figure out how to keep them down so I can penetrate her heart.

Their heart.

CHAPTER FIVE

Chloe

T HE SUN WAKES ME SLOWLY, SHINING THROUGH THE CRACKED window that has yet to be replaced. It's warm, just like the arm wrapped around me, holding me tight. It feels good. My soul is settled. There is a part of me that always fights, always rebels, and is always needing *more*.

But right now, my rebellion is quiet, and the static inside my mind is muted.

I dare to say, I feel peace.

The arm around me tightens, and the random touch pulls me out of my thoughts and daydreams. I look down to the familiar devil on his arm staring back at me, and I yelp. Jerking out of his hold, I roll away, falling right onto the unforgiving floor.

I land right on my back with a thud. My tailbone

screams in pain slithering up my spine. "Owie," I say, holding my breath.

"Chloe? Fuck. Are you okay?" the man from yesterday looks down from the bed. His beard is pointing in different directions and his eyes are still full of sleep. He rubs them to wake up, and he crawls across the bed until he slides off the edge and joins me. Zain lays down beside me and we both stare at the ceiling. "This would be a lot more comfortable on the bed, you know."

"You startled me when I woke up. I didn't plan on falling off the bed. Your floor is hard, by the way. My tailbone hurts."

"Floors are usually hard," he chuckles, and then his hand slides down my arm, awakening my skin just like the sun wakes the world when it rises.

His hand slides into mine, and I inhale a sharp breath when he intertwines our fingers. I need to pull away. I don't know this man. He's just someone I met last night.

But when I try to unlock our fingers, he squeezes tighter, not allowing me to leave.

"I'm not going to hurt you, Chloe. You're as safe as you can ever be with me."

"I don't know you," I whisper, swallowing the nerves building up in my throat. "This is happening so fast. I'm not used to doing things like this. Jessica doesn't speak for me. I'm not her—"

He rolls on top of me, and I push my head back to try and get away from him, but the damn floors stop me. "You don't think I know that?" He lifts a hand to my face, cradling my jaw with his massive palm.

Like an idiot, I lean into him instead of fighting him and let out a heavy breath. Why does he feel so good?

"I know you're nothing like her. I respect that. My goal isn't to have only one of you, Chloe."

My eyes flutter open, and I'm casted into rich brown eyes, sparking against the sun's rays like a rare gem. "What's your goal, then?" I ask, afraid of his answer as I lick my dry lips.

His eyes hood just as his thumb brushes over the apple of my cheek. "To have both of you," he admits.

He must see the shock on my face. No one wants me. I'm not the woman people want. I'm crazy. I'm a burden. Who would deal with someone who has two personalities? He must be lying. I push against his chest to get him off me. "That isn't funny!" I yell, tears pooling and impairing my vision, as if I've had one too many drinks. "That isn't—"

"—Do you see me laughing, sweet girl?" His thumb trails along my jaw, gathering the tear that fell from the corner of my eye.

He lifts his thumb against the light and the small water droplet reflects before he sucks his finger into his mouth. His eyes close, and he groans as he tastes my tears.

I need to be afraid. I need to run.

But something tells me if I tried to escape, he'd chase me.

And it scares me as much as it turns me on.

When he opens his eyes again, he leans down, his lips becoming too close to mine. I've forgotten how to breathe.

"Have you ever kissed a man before, Chloe?" he asks, his words a warm caress across my mouth.

I shake my head, unable to speak as I wonder if he is about to do what I think he is.

"Good. That's real good, sweet girl." His palm moves to my neck, his fingers lacing around my nape to hold me in place.

"Why?" I croak, my throat dry as my body comes alive from his teasing. Is this teasing? He's between my legs. I can feel the strength of his body pressing me against the floor and the hard ridge of his cock against my thigh.

It's the closest I've ever been with a man, and I'm not sure what to do. I'm afraid to move, to breathe, to speak, but I don't think I want him to leave.

His presence is intoxicating. The kind a woman can get addicted to if she isn't careful, and if I know myself, I'm far from careful.

Not because of me, but because of *her*.

"Because these lips are mine, sweet girl. Mine and mine alone." He turns his head, brushing his bottom lip against mine, and my lips part from the electric touch. I remember to take a breath, and he holds me still as he teases me again, his thumb tracing the outline of my mouth.

I want to ask him why he wants to kiss me now, but when he had a chance to have sex with Jessica last night, he didn't. My mind fogs up the closer his mouth gets to mine. My tongue is tied like a knot in a rope, and I can't speak.

"Fucking beautiful," he whispers in admiration as he closes the distance between us. His mouth meets mine, and

I freeze. I have no idea what to do. I close my eyes and do my best to kiss him back. There's no tongue, not yet. Our lips are sealed and moving in sync without getting carried away.

Yet, I'm getting carried away, anyhow.

He groans into my mouth, deepening the kiss and opening my lips more, diving into me, accepting me.

All of me.

I'd thought I had a person who accepted me, but I was wrong.

This is acceptance.

And it terrifies me.

I wrap my arms around his back, my fingers digging into the thick muscle of his shoulders, and whimper as I feel the tip of his tongue testing my lips. Before I can know what he truly tastes like, he brings the kiss to a slow stop. His lips are softer than what I imagine a cloud is like. It's a complete contradiction to what he looks like. All big, burly, and muscular. I expect his lips to be just as rough and demanding as he seems.

But they aren't.

They treat me delicately, with a fragile passion that I want to get lost in.

"Your lips are the heaven I've been seeking from a lifetime of living in hell, Chloe," he confesses, brushing his mouth across mine again.

I stay quiet because I don't know what to say. I don't want to ruin the moment. I don't know what I'm feeling. I'm confused, because I hardly know Zain, but I want to get to know him more. My body is on fire, my lips tingle, and my heart is racing to the point that I think it might explode.

"What the fuck happened to my bike?" a deep voice booms in the house, nearly shaking the walls.

"Damn it," Zain curses and rolls off me. A rush of cold air replaces the warmth of his body heat. I miss it. He grabs my hands and helps me to my feet. My head swims from standing too fast—or maybe it was the earth-shattering kiss, who knows?

"Are you okay? You fell and hit the ground pretty hard, and I attacked you," he chuckles.

"I'm perfect," I say breathlessly, staring at his swollen lips. "I... is... was that okay?" I ask, nervous that maybe the kiss wasn't good enough. He should have kissed me while I was Jessica. She wouldn't question a kiss. She'd take it, own it, and show whoever's kissing her that she is the boss.

"Are you kidding? Best first kiss of my life," he grins, pulling me toward him by wrapping a hand around my waist. He kisses my forehead and sighs. "I hope you know you can't go anywhere," he says, a hint of a threat on the ends of his words as his voice deepens.

Before I can ask how I'm his first kiss, he walks to the chair cattycornered against the wall and picks up the clothes he got me last night. "Change really quick, and we will head out to the living room to explain to Tool what happened to his bike."

I blush when I remember the crash of the heavy metal yanked me back to reality. "I happened to his bike."

"I'm going to take the blame."

"I can't have you do that," I say quickly, holding the clothes to my chest. I almost don't want to take off the robe because it's so soft, but I can't meet people wearing this. "It was my fault. I have to take responsibility." I head toward the bathroom and then think, why bother? He's already seen me naked. But the thought of taking off my clothes has my skin crawling. A kiss is one thing, showing my body is another.

"It wasn't you that hit the bike," he insists, wrapping his fingers around my wrist before I can open the bathroom door. "I know what it's like not to be yourself. It was Jessica who hit the bike, not you."

"Doesn't matter," I tell him, pulling my wrist away from his hold. "It's me. I'm her."

"You're not her. You're nothing like her."

"Why are you doing this? Why are you so calm about this? I don't have friends. I've never had a lover. Never thought I would, yet here you are, ready to take on two types of crazy? What the hell are you doing? Am I a joke to you?" I stare down at my feet, trying to gather my thoughts. I know if I don't calm down, I'll black out and won't remember a thing until Jessica leaves.

"What? You're far from a joke. I first saw you and I knew I wanted you for myself, Chloe."

"It wasn't me you saw!" I yell, the words catching on a sob. "No one wants someone with so much baggage."

"Don't you dare talk about yourself like that." He slams me against the bathroom door and his shoulders roll. His face turns red. The vein his forehead travels up his bald head and he slams his fist against the door, shaking the wood against my spine. "You have no idea how perfect you are. You were made me for me," he raises his voice just as he cracks his neck, the pops of his joints causing my skin to pebble.

"I want to take the both of you and hide you away," he says. "Make it so that the only man you see is me. The only one you will crave... is me." He wraps a hand around my throat, not squeezing, but enough to turn me on and freak me out. "You think you walked inside an old asylum and thought you were the only one with problems?" He brings his lips my ear, his tongue flicking across my earlobe. "We are all insane here, sweet girl."

"And what's your insanity?" I ask him, hoping he will tell me.

"I'm staring at it," he growls, shoving his lips against mine again, his hand tightening around my throat.

He rips his lips from mine, and I blink, running my thumb across my lip. "Why don't you put your head between my legs and show me what that mouth can really do?"

"Jessica."

"Long time no see, lover boy." I nip at his lip, but he pulls away, leaving me to pout. "So you can have all the fun with her and not me? That hurts my feelings."

"You know what I think?" He squeezes my throat harder, his thumb pressing against the jugular vein, and I moan. "I think this is a front. No doubt you're dominant, but I think you're just as scared as Chloe is in some way. I'm gaining her trust before I gain yours. I want talk to Chloe."

"She's not here right now."

"Chloe!" he shouts, grabbing the sides of my face and staring with his beautiful eyes.

Damn him for knowing to call out her name.

CHAPTER SIX

Zain

I READ SOMEWHERE THAT IF YOU CALL OUT THE ORIGINAL personality's name, they usually answer. Jessica doesn't seem too happy with me, but I wasn't kidding when I said I wanted to gain the trust of Chloe first. Jessica is a firecracker, while Chloe is a slow burning fire that has no idea how strong she is.

Jessica explodes when she makes herself known, but Chloe has just begun to fuel her wild blaze. I have no doubt she's slowly going to own the world, turning it to ash as time goes on.

"You don't want me? You want her?"

The rejection grows on Jessica's face and the wind in her tough sails are gone.

"Hey, look at me," I say, grabbing her by the shoulders.

"I want both of you, but I have a feeling Chloe needs more time than you do. She's the bigger part of you, and that's the part I need, or this will never work. But make no mistake, I want you both." I lay a kiss on her lips, and it's different than kissing Chloe.

Chloe is timid and unsure, while Jessica is fierce and dominant. She grabs me by my shirt, fisting the material as she yanks me closer to deepen the kiss. She lashes out her tongue first, sliding it against mine. She bites my lip, sucking it into her mouth before letting it go with a plop.

Fuck yes, I love not knowing what I'm going to get with her.

"You sure you want Chloe, right now? Feels like you want me." Jessica cups my cock over my flimsy pajama pants, wrapping her fingers around me.

"I want both of you, but give me Chloe, Jessica. I'll deal with you later," I say. It comes out harsher than I intend it to but I'm hanging on by a thread. I want nothing more than to pull my pants down and watch her jack me off. I want to watch as I spill my seed in her hand coating her palm. Then, I want to watch her lick herself clean, swallowing my come and getting every drop so it doesn't go to waste.

"Promise?" She puts on a good show, but I see the question in her eyes, the fear of being rejected and ignored for Chloe.

"Oh, I never make promises I can't keep, sweet girl."

She presses her lips against mine again, rough and wild with a hint of madness, just how I like it. I grab the back of her head, pouring my promise inside her so she knows I'm serious, when the kiss slows. The heat is still there, the electric shock still connects us, but the confidence and certainty is gone.

Chloe is back, not questioning why she is kissing me, but is kissing me anyway.

These women are going to be the death of me.

I break the kiss, staring at her in awe, and push her hair back so I can see her face. "You kept kissing me anyway," I offer.

The small, coy smirk dances on her lips as she blushes again. She tilts her head down, twisting her fingers in all sorts of directions from nerves. "I think if there is one thing Jessica and I can agree on, it's kissing you. I wasn't surprised to come back and find my lips attached to yours. Jessica can't help herself."

"How about you?" I ask, wrapping a piece of her blonde hair around my finger. It's like spun gold. The riches of the world are in every strand, and I consider myself a wealthy man for even being allowed to touch the silky locks. "Can you help yourself?"

She slides the bathroom door behind her and takes a step back. "I'm working on it," she says, giving me a tease of her hazel eyes before she shuts the door.

I grip the edges of the trim on either side of the doorway and hang my head. I'm so fucking in love. Holy shit.

I have to marry her. I won't be able to breathe, to function, to think, not until this need to have her as mine and only mine is met. And even then, I don't think it will be enough. Many dangerous thoughts run through my mind when I think of Chloe and Jessica.

For one, if I can't have her, no one can.

Two, if she doesn't want me, I'll have to kill her.

And then I'll have to kill myself, because I know I'm not going to be able to live in a world without her.

She has no idea who I am. It's only fair I tell her soon, not that she'll have a choice in the matter. If she doesn't like me for my mania, she'll have to learn, because she isn't going anywhere where I can't see her, feel her, touch her, smell her, or hear her voice.

I know she can learn to love me.

Someone can love anyone if they are given the time.

She has to.

It's for her own good.

My thoughts are racing. I run my hand over my head and count to three. My heart pounds like a drum, thudding against my chest with constant heavy rhythm. I'm waiting for my sternum to crack and my heart to crawl from my chest and fall onto the floor. I'd watch in horror and in fascination, as with every lingering beat the jinxed organ tries to crawl to her.

She has no idea just how far I've fallen. How blurred the lines of right and wrong have become. I no longer know the difference. As long as she is here, whether locked in a padded room, or happy sitting on the couch, she's here.

That's all I need.

"Are you okay?" she asks as she opens the bathroom door.

Sweat drips from the top of my head, flowing down behind my ear and to my neck. "I'm fine," I croak, trying to control the edge of madness piercing my mind with its talons. She has no idea how much I want to whisk her away, and the fact that I care enough not to is what is causing my body to burn. "Let's go explain ourselves to Tool, yeah?" I say, wiping my cheek on my shoulder to dry the sweat. It's embarrassing.

I hold out my hand, hoping she takes it, and without hesitation she slips her fingers between mine. I lock them in place so she can't pull away and drag her toward the door. "You look beautiful, by the way." Her pajama top is tighter around her breasts; a simple t-shirt, nothing special about it.

Only the fact that she is wearing it makes it the most expensive and wanted material in my world. I'd kill anyone to have that shirt, just so I can smell it when she isn't around. I'd wrap it around my cock and let the knowledge that she wore it bring me to orgasm.

The pajama pants are the spandex kind, stopping right below her knee and hugging every shape of her body. God, she's fucking perfect.

I know she thinks she's found sanctuary here, but this house is haunted, and she's danced

right into a nightmare.

I fling the door open so hard it smashes against the wall, and Chloe tenses her grip in my hand. "What the fuck do you want, Tool?" I snap impatiently. My head is pounding. I rub the side of my head.

"The mirror on my bike is broken. Do you know how

that happened?" He crosses his arms over his chest, his tattoos moving across his biceps as he flexes. He stares at Chloe and lifts his chin. "Who is she? When did she get here?"

"None of your fucking business," I sneer, keeping Chloe behind me so no one can look at her. Maybe having her meet everyone was a mistake. I need to take her downstairs. She'd understand. Maybe not now, but one day.

"It is my business. Especially if she had something to do with my bike."

"Don't even fucking look at her! She's mine, Tool. Mine!" I shove his chest and my vision tunnels until all I see is him in my line of sight. I'm going to kill him. "She's mine. Only mine. Forever. She belongs to me. I'll kill anyone who looks at her wrong. Do you understand?"

"Touch me again," Tool growls between irate, shaking breaths. "And you will see just what I can do with this screwdriver. Reaper's uncle or not. No one fucking touches me like that. And I don't give a fuck about your piece of ass, Zain. I care about my bike."

I launch myself at Tool and wrap my hands around his throat. The mania takes over. I see nothing. I feel everything. All I need is to banish the threat from our lives and Chloe and I can live happily ever after. Another drop of sweat makes it way down to my face, stopping at my lip. I flick my tongue out, gathering the bead as if it were fuel.

"She isn't a piece of ass. She's my forever. Do you understand me?!" I lift his head off the ground and growl, snapping the air with my teeth when his face his close enough. The energy grows in my face. "You need to listen to me! Listen!" I shake him as I yell and he coughs, slapping my forearms with his hands, but I'm desperate for someone to listen to me. "No one listens to me. You need to understand."

"Zain," Chloe's sweet voice has me turning my head to her. She's against the wall, covering her mouth with her palm. She doesn't like what she sees. I've scared her.

Good.

She needs to know what her life is going to be like being around a man like me. It isn't going to be rainbows and puppies.

More like flames and a ride over broken nails.

I scream when something stabs my thigh. I let go of Tool's throat and look down to see a screwdriver sticking out of my leg. He rubs his neck and gasps for air. "You crazy fucking bastard. You need to calm the fuck down. I don't want your woman. I have my own and she sings me to fucking sleep every night because she has a voice of a sparrow. God, get your shit together."

"He can't," Reaper says from the doorway, setting a box down onto the floor. "Are you okay, Tool?"

"I'm fine. I just want to know what happened to my bike, and he went fucking ballistic on me." Tool rubs his throat, then bends down and yanks his screwdriver from my leg. "I have a feeling there is a lot I don't know. If I'm in a mad house, I deserve to know all the fucking details."

"It was me," Chloe says, her body language timid as she wraps her arms around herself. I hobble over to her, wincing from the annoying pain in my leg. "I—" and like a flip of a switch, her arms unfold and she pushes off the wall, confident and sexy. She slings her hair over her shoulder as she begins to dance down the hall, twirling like she did last night in the desert. "I was dancing and bumped into your bike."

"What the hell were you doing in the middle of the desert?" Tool asks her.

I sag against the wall, soaked with sweat, and slide down until I hit the floor. I'm exhausted.

Jessica gives one last twirl, and when she sees me on the ground, she runs over to me, sliding on her knees across the floor. "I'm sorry, but I can't tell you that. It's a secret." She runs her hand over my cheek, and I hum, loving her touch. But then just as quickly as she appeared, Jessica is gone.

"Are you okay? What happened?" Chloe asks, her brows furrowed in that cute confusion she gets when she comes back from the dark. "You're bleeding," she gasps. "We need a first aid kit."

"Okay," Tool laughs, then lets out a breath that's half chuckle, half sigh. "What the hell was that? And what do you mean it's a secret?"

"What secret? What are you talking about?" Chloe doesn't turn around to ask Tool.

"You said you were dancing in the desert, and I asked why, then you said you wouldn't tell me, because it's a secret."

"I don't have any secrets," she muses, taking the first aid kit from Reaper. She lays her hand on my shoulder and she inhales a sharp breath. "You're burning up and you are sweating buckets."

"Yeah, when I come down from an episode it's like I got hit by a bus," I say, fighting the need to sleep for three days.

"An episode?" she questions, lifting a perfectly groomed brow at me. "You have something to tell me."

"Everyone has something to tell me! I'm confused as fuck and no one is giving me answers," Tool gripes. "I nearly died because of your 'episode'. I deserve to know. And you better share you secrets. Secrets don't make friends here, they bring war. So spill." Tool mumbles something else under his breath as he strides to the kitchen. He turns on the faucet and washes the blood off his screwdriver. "Everyone deserves to know the shit we are getting into."

"Tool, that's enough. I'll let you know what I want you to know," Reaper snaps. His boots clobber the floor as he strolls over to me, his cut gleaming in the living room light. When he gets to me, he squats, pushing my leg to the side to get a better look at the wound.

"Hey, be careful with him," Chloe says, smacking Reaper's hand.

He chuckles. "Sorry, my mistake. I'm used to a lot worse, is all. You okay, Uncle Zain?" he asks me.

"Yeah, that's not what hurts," I reply. My head feels like it's going to explode, like a bull with horns is ramming against my skull.

"Tool is right, Zain. Until I have all the information on

you and everyone you live with, I can't help you anymore. I won't risk the life of my members. Okay?"

"I know."

He turns to Chloe, who ignores him and stares at me, grasping my hand harder the longer Reaper stares at her. "Why don't you know the secret?" he asks.

Her eyes dart to the side and her chest rises and falls with quicker breaths. "I need to know."

"Chloe, it's okay," I tell her as she cleans the screwdriver puncture in my leg with rubbing alcohol. "You can trust him."

"But can I?"

"Damn it, Jessica," I grit my teeth and thud my head against the wall.

"You just said her name was Chloe."

"Surprise," Jessica laughs. "I'm her better half, Jessica." She holds out a hand toward Reaper and he reciprocates with a slow handshake.

"Chloe," I say her name again, and Jessica whirls her head so fast her hair twirls just like she does when she dances.

"You're always wanting her."

"Chloe," I growl at Jessica.

"Heads up, Chloe doesn't know the secret. I do. And I'll make sure to protect us. I'm never going to say a word. That you can count on. The both of you." She lets go of Reaper's hand, and when those hazel eyes land on me, I know it's Chloe. "So sorry, I don't know what secret you're talking about, but I do have a split personality. The other can be real bitch, so sorry in advance. Or so I've heard anyway," she mumbles, giving Reaper a grim expression. She tears my new pajama pants to make room for the bandage and sticks it on. "There. All done."

"Holy hell, you lot are going to put us through the ringer. What a mind fuck," Reaper glowers, then rubs a hand down his face. "Okay. That's fine. Everything is fine." He takes a deep breath and lowers his hands to the ground, then up toward the sky as he exhales, and repeats the process until he is settled.

"I know we have a lot to talk about, but do you care if it waits? I'm exhausted, and I really need to sleep. After a manic attack, I get into a depressive slump. It's natural."

"Yeah, if you need anything, let me know. I'll be hiring a nurse. Today. Whether you like it or not. You understand?" It's not a question, but an order. I know that even if I fight him on it, I know he will go and hire a nurse anyway.

"Part time, okay? We need our freedom."

"We'll see. We will finish up some restorations today. You rest. I'm going to go check on Porter to see if I want to kill him or not."

"Tongue won't like that, Prez," Tool pipes up. "If someone is going to kill his brother, it should be him."

"Goddamn it, this fucking world just keeps spinning faster. I mean, who the fuck else deals with shit like this?" Reaper kicks the screen door open and lets out a frustrated howl-like sound. "Damn it!" He kicks the beam, then hops on one leg. "That hurt! My god, I knew I should have worn my steel-toed boots today. Damn everything to hell. Everything. All of it."

Tool snickers as he watches Reaper, then schools his features when we catch him. "It isn't often he feels like this. I like to experience it."

I have a feeling Reaper would kill him if he found out Tool laughed at him.

"Come on." Chloe wraps her slender arm around my waist. "Let's get you to bed."

"Are you going to stay with me?" I ask, using the wall as leverage to stand up.

"If you speak truths," she says, carrying some of my weight as we walk back to my bedroom.

Truths.

In some ways, they are nearly as bad as lies.

At least in a lie, you get what you want. In truths, you're usually left alone with guilt and regret.

I can't lie to Chloe.

All I can do is hope she accepts me like I've accepted her.

All of me or none of me.

It's only my heart at stake.

CHAPTER SEVEN

Chloe

All eyes are on me as I help walk Zain to his bedroom. I feel like we are never going to make it out of that damn room with how much time we spend in it. I have more questions than I do answers right now, no thanks to Jessica. I'm already making enemies because of her. I don't think it's a good idea to get on a biker's bad side, especially the President of the club.

Most of my life has been hectic because of Jessica. I remember when I was a teenager and I started having blackouts. It caused so much turmoil between me and my parents. I wouldn't remember anything about a conversation I had with them, which apparently usually ended up with me cursing them or sneaking out. It wasn't me, it was Jessica.

I only remembered waking up in my bed the next day.

They would say it was an excuse. I was making things up so I wouldn't have a punishment, but I was truly lost. Eventually, my parents got tired of my antics and sent me to a therapist.

That's when my personality named herself.

It took me ages to accept the fact I had someone else inside my head. I didn't want to be crazy. I wanted a normal life, but that wasn't in the cards for me, even with medication. My parents felt terrible for treating me so harshly whey they found out I had been telling the truth. I really didn't remember cussing them out. I don't remember sneaking out and doing god-knows-what, because it wasn't me.

I've learned to live with her. What choice do I have? And I've yet to find a person that likes Jessica. She's a floozy little bitch that only exists to make my life more complicated. Well, there is Zain. I'm not sure what his intentions are. I'm not sure if I'm a joke or a challenge to him, but I like that he likes me.

And not just me. Her too.

For some reason.

"Thank you," Zain says as he unwraps his arm from my waist and falls to the bed. His face is pale, his shirt is soaked from sweat, and he has dark circles under his eyes. It's like he ran a marathon, even if it only lasted ten minutes.

"I'll draw you a bath. Consider it me returning the favor from last night."

"Are you going to join me?" he asks, his voice raspy and delicious as he pushes into an up-right position.

"I... I don't know. I don't think that's a good idea. I know it doesn't really matter because of Jessica, since she showed off our body like it was meant to be on display in some mall—"

"—You are meant to be on display, but not for everyone to see, Chloe. Just me. I'll admire you, but I won't touch you, not until you're ready."

"I don't know you," I say. That's a good reason not to get in a tub with a stranger.

"Let's change that, sweet girl. I'll take a quick shower instead. You and I can put on a movie in here since I don't have cable."

"What about everyone out there?"

"What about them?" he asks, limping by me to get to the bathroom.

"I... well... you..." I stumble over my words to try and find a good explanation and point to the door. "I think it's the right thing to do. I'm a stranger."

"This isn't the place to give a damn about the right thing, sweet girl."

"There is always a place for the right thing, regardless of circumstance." He looks at me over his shoulder, those sultry brows soaking into me like a warm fire on a cold night. I've missed nights in front of the fireplace at home with my parents. The desert nights are cold, which make a perfect reason to light a fire.

He straightens and slips off his shirt, then his torn pants, and I gasp when I see him naked. I glance away as quick as I can, my cheeks as hot as a summer Vegas day. There is no doubt that he is a good-looking man. And big.

Everywhere.

I cross my arms over my chest and hear him chuckle before he steps into the shower stall, the frosted glass blurring out his body enough that I can breathe and look his way again. He has his hurt leg out of the stall door, so it doesn't get wet. I leave him be instead of talking to him. Being around Zain gets me flustered and nervous.

I've never been good around people. Jessica is better at that. She's outgoing and fun, while I'm introverted and quiet. I never had friends in school, especially when I started blacking out. Apparently, while Jessica was fun, she wasn't too likeable.

Go figure.

And then I was the crazy girl.

My mom pulled me out of school eventually, and I finished high school being homeschooled. The majority of my life has been this narrowing tunnel, and I've been jogging toward the end where the damn light is, but it gets further away with every step I take.

Jessica is the tunnel.

My sanity is the light.

I walk away and take one last look at him in the shower, a parting glance. Jessica must have rubbed off on me a bit. There's a corner of the stall that isn't frosted, and I can see everything. He has a hand against the beige tile of the shower stall, his head dropped, and the water beats down between his shoulder blades. I take a step forward, drawn to him like a moth to a flame. The water uses the divot of his spine to flow down his body. My eyes follow the river until I'm staring at his bubbled butt. I almost squeak when he turns around and tilts his head back so he can get it wet. I cover my mouth with my hands and ravage his body with my eyes.

Hell in a handbasket, he makes it hard to resist him when he's as hot as the flames he was born in.

Zain's body is strong, thick, and hairy, just like a man should be—a real man. He is nothing like Dr. Washington, my therapist. He was one of the only men I had been around besides my father, and I had grown so attached to him that I fell in love with him. I don't find myself missing him though, so it must not have been real love. Zain makes me feel more than Dr. Washington ever did, and I saw my therapist three times a week for so many years I lost count.

I devour Zain with my eyes, holding a hand over my heart, feeling it thump wildly against my chest. He shakes his head and runs his hand down his face, then his neck, and runs his fingers through his chest hair.

I want to do that.

My fingers twitch to touch him, and when his hand wraps around his thick cock and cups his heavy orbs, a gush of liquid lust wets my panties.

It's erotic. Even if he is covered in suds, he's still the most attractive man I've ever seen.

But what's his fight? What does he fall victim to? It's obvious he does. You don't have really high highs and then crash and burn for no reason.

It takes crazy to know crazy. Maybe that's why I'm so comfortable around him.

He turns around again, giving me his back, and I take

that moment to rip my eyes away from the rolling muscles and hurry to the bed. My nipples are hard and the space between my legs is throbbing with heat. I feel so foolish for being like this. Just because I've never been with a man before doesn't mean I'm a prude.

Why would I want to be with anyone that didn't understand me or accept me? I had enough rumors going around when I was in my teens. I didn't want to be the 'crazy girl' guys conquered because they made a bet with their friends.

There were a few close calls, but Jessica swooped in and saved my ass.

"You okay?" he asks.

I'm startled when I realize I've been staring at the floor. When I divert my attention to Zain, he tucks the towel around his waist.

I gulp.

Listen, not only am I a woman, I have another woman living inside me. It's like a double dose of lust and arousal all at once.

His cock.

Is there.

Pressing against the towel.

I can see the outline of it. All of it.

Including the helmet of the head.

"You keep looking at me like that, we won't be talking, sweet girl. And I have a feeling, you're the type that needs to talk before you spread those legs."

"I will not be spreading my legs for you or anyone. You

be careful with how you talk to me." I try to sound stern and offended, but I'm breathless and winded.

Especially when he closes the distance between us and tilts my head back. He stares down at me, his jaw set hard. The exhaustion in his eyes is still there but enflamed with rage. Zain's hand lands on my leg and I take a second to see if he tries to move up my thigh, but he doesn't. There is a skull tattooed beneath his knuckles, with butterfly wings on either side. It promises death and beauty all at once, which seems fitting, considering he holds the complex nature of both really well.

Zain is a concoction of misnomers and contradictions, but still, I yearn for the deranged brew to course through my system. Maybe he's poison; and will kill me slowly or maybe he's the best damn thing I'll ever have.

He grips my chin, and the hold is tight, almost punishing, and his thumb rubs against my bottom lip. The air cools against my teeth before he pops my lip into place. "Make no mistake, Chloe, you're going to spread your legs for me. It might not be today or tomorrow—" His lips are a fraction of an inch away from mine, sucking the air out of my lungs "—But I will find myself inside that virgin cunt of yours. I'm going to own it just like I'm going to own you, because you're mine, sweet girl. All fucking mine. And if you even try to leave me, I will throw you in a padded room. I'm obsessed. And a man like me, a man of my condition, it is much more intense than someone normal will ever feel."

"So—" I flick my tongue out and taste the tip of his

thumb. A hint of soap is lingering on his skin. "—I need to be afraid of you."

"Yes," he teases my lips with his.

"Are you going to hurt me?"

"No."

"Do you want me to be afraid of you?"

"No," he says, shaking his head, tickling my mouth with his beard.

"Why me?"

"My mania chose you."

"What's mania?" I'm almost afraid to ask, but just because I have a mental disorder doesn't mean I know all of them.

He crawls over me, causing me to lay against the mattress. "Periods of extremely high moods or elevated excitement. My sex drive—" he grabs my ribcage and kisses the middle of chest "—increases. The need to release the energy becomes paramount."

"Tell me more," I say as he hovers over me. I'm surprised Jessica hasn't taken over since he admitted to wanting to lock me away, but I don't think she's afraid of him or she would have made herself known. I'm going to trust her.

Something I'll never say again.

I lay my hand against his cheek, then run my fingers through his beard. "I want to know everything, so I understand you. I think it's fair. You've seen the other side of me, and you've seen me naked. Those are two things I don't share with people."

"I can remedy both of those right now," he jokes, his

hand flying to the tie of his towel. "I'm kidding." He lays his hand on my hip and slides it up my side, outlining the sides of my breast. "I know what you want."

Zain doesn't say it with excitement. I mean, no one likes talking about the part of them that makes them imperfect. He slides off me, landing on his side, and props his head up on his chin. "What do you want to know, sweet girl?"

I mimic his position and rub my fingers across his skin, tracing the devil on his arm. I don't know why I like it so much. Maybe it's because I think it fits him so well. "What happened with Tool?"

"Yeah," he nods. "That's a manic episode. Rapid thinking, risky behaviors, random ideas, anger, thoughts of suicide, grandiosity, hostility. It's associated with bipolar disorder."

"Does that happen often?"

"It gets really agitated when I'm feeling emotional. I try to keep it under control, but it's like, well... it's like the devil comes out," he says, looking down at his tattoo. I understand why he has it now. "When I was a kid, I didn't know how to control it. I would explode and beat some other kid to a pulp, then come to my senses only after the damage had been done. They locked me away for it."

I nod, understanding him more, the way he thinks and speaks. "And your so-called obsession? Is that part of it?"

"No," he says, rolling on top of me again. "That has to with thirty-five years of living in a twelve by ten room. If anything, it made certain aspects of my mania worse." He yawns. "I'm sorry. I usually get really tired after an episode."

"No, it's okay. I understand."

"If I wake up and find you gone, I'm going to lock you away. I'm not kidding," He wraps an arm around me and tugs me against his body. "From now on, wherever I go, you go. And tomorrow, we're getting married." He shuts his eyes, and in a matter of seconds he falls asleep.

I blink quickly at him, speechless and taken aback. Marriage? I don't even know his middle name!

Now my mind starts to race, and I think about all of his symptoms.

What if that's what I am? A symptom?

I can't marry someone because their illness tells them they have to. I don't want to be a byproduct of his mania. Marriage is hectic enough without adding the crazy aspect to it.

I have to get out of here.

For his sake.

But not for mine.

Because even knowing I need to be afraid, I know his mania wanting me is more love than I'll ever get from someone for as long as I live.

People like me, we aren't meant for happy endings.

We sabotage them.

CHAPTER EIGHT

Chloe

I WAKE UP WITH A START, CURSING MYSELF FOR FALLING ASLEEP. Zain's heavy arm is over me, nearly crushing my chest with its weight. Carefully, I lift the massive limb off me and roll away. My feet land on the floor, and I take one last look at Zain. He is on his stomach, one arm under the pillow and other by his side. The towel found its way off sometime in the night. It hangs off the bed, right under his hips. His right butt-cheek is showing, the sheet barely covering his naked body.

I'm going to miss him more than I should. I barely know the man, but it's like the worst part of me yearns for the worst part of him, and the good part of me knows better.

We could never work.

People like us? We're stuck dreaming. And dreams don't make a good reality.

"Bye, Zain," I whisper, leaning down to kiss his shiny, bald head. I inhale his scent, the pine soap lingering on his skin.

Why does my heart ache more than it should? I've known him two days. That isn't long enough to love someone.

My crazy is drawn to his, that's all this is.

I'm a symptom for his mania to quench. Nothing more, nothing less. I can't have this going further. I'll end up getting hurt because I know I'll fall in love with him. I fall in love easy, just ask my therapist.

Before I leave, I grab his shirt on the floor and bring it my nose, tears prickling my eyes. I'll take it with me. Something to remember him by. I have to. I clutch the simple grey shirt to my chest and tiptoe toward the door. I turn the knob and step through the doorway and peer over the curve of my shoulder to have one last look at the man that's changed… something inside me. Even the part of me that I don't get along with. The darkness that always takes me is quieter.

I close the door and gasp when I nearly run into a chest.

"Hi. Hi. Hi." A man I haven't met before says three times. I can't believe I've been in this house for two days and the only people I've met are damn bikers. "I'm Oli. Who are you? Zain didn't say he had company."

"I'm Chloe," I reply and try to sidestep him, but he follows.

"I made breakfast. Do you want any?" his voice is deep, and his ink-colored hair hangs in his eyes.

"No, thank you. I'm just leaving now. It's nice to meet you, Oli."

"You are leaving? Does Zain know you're going? He doesn't like it when people leave."

"It's alright, Oli," Reaper, the man from yesterday says, as he props his hip against the granite countertop in the kitchen. "She's her own woman. If she wants to go, she can go. I'll have Tool take you wherever you want to go." He lifts an olive green mug and takes a sip out of it. By the smell, I'd say it's coffee. His hand makes the damn cup look tiny. One good squeeze and it will break.

"I can go?" I frown, surprised that it would be so easy.

"I think Zain has enough on his plate, to be honest," Reaper says.

"This is uncomfortable. I'm going to leave." Oli starts to walk one way, then turns on his heel to go in another direction. "It's this way. Bye. Bye. Bye," he says, scurrying down the hall.

We fall into a thick cloud of awkward silence. "I care about him."

Reaper's lips are nearly touching the rim of his cup and he laughs, but the way it sounds rubs me the wrong way. "Listen Chloe, I'm sure you're a nice girl, but in case you haven't noticed, this isn't Disney World. You obviously have a choice to fit in here, but Zain and his crew still need to settle in, and the last thing Zain needs is to get attached to someone who isn't serious about him. The people here are fragile—"

I take a step forward and have to hold back my anger at the too familiar word. "They are stronger than you think. They are not fragile," I spit and march my way over to the front door. "We are stronger than you," I say, my hand gripping the doorknob. "Because while you battle what you need to wear every day, we battle more, and somehow manage to live a life in the same world you're in. Don't ever call us fragile. I do care about him, it's why I'm leaving. I don't want to be a symptom of his mania. I don't want to be a regret when the fog clears, or he wakes up one day and realizes what he has done."

Reaper reaches into his back pocket just as Tool comes around the corner, his shirt covered in paint. "Damn it. Oli went and slammed the damned door, having no idea that I was using it as a support to paint. Knocked me off the ladder and paint went everywhere."

"Sorry. Sorry. Sorry," Oli runs around the corner, skidding across the floor and dragging white smears down the hall trying to stop.

Reaper's focus switches gears, and I take the moment to slip out the door. The air is cool, and the clouds are heavy in the sky, tinting the desert gloomy grey. I throw on Zain's shirt, swallowing the emotion when his scent drifts to my nostrils. I don't know where I'm going, but I'll figure it out, just like I always do.

I run down the steps as the breeze kicks up sand, twirling it around in a small tornado before vanishing along the desert floor. There isn't much around here, just some trees and bushes. It's hard to see which way is the exit, since everything looks the same.

Bush.

Bush.

Dead bush.

Sand.

Bush again.

Oh, now there is something new.

Tire tracks.

"Where'd she go?" I hear Reaper shout from the house.

Before he can catch me, I run, slithering through the bikes and trucks. My feet land in the strip of the tire imprint. The ridges of the tread push against my feet, causing a slight edge of pain. I can't stop. The feeling of running away feels familiar, the rush of adrenaline in hopes I don't get caught.

But why?

The grumble of bikes shakes the ground, and I pump my arms for an extra burst of speed.

"I don't care what it takes! Fucking find her. Now!" Reaper yells loudly over the rowdy engines.

I take a sharp right before I get to the road and jump over bushes and rocks. Damn it, I wish I had shoes. I wince when I land on something sharp, causing me to stumble. I barely catch myself, and my palms skid across the pebbles, scraping roughly against the ground. I hiss, biting back the pain, and stumble upright until I'm running again. I'm sweating, the muscles in my thighs trembling from exertion. The edge of the forest is near, but when the horsepower of the Harleys quicken, I dive behind a boulder, hoping it hides me for the most part.

But the bikes get further away instead of closer.

I peek over the rock and run to the edge of the road, look left, then right, watching them turn into small dots in the distance.

Well, at least they are going the wrong way. It gives me time to figure out… something.

The asphalt vibrates under my feet. The grill of a truck comes to view, and I hold out my thumb, walking backward along the side of the road. My teeth chatter from the cold, and all I can do is hope the person behind the wheel won't let a girl walk this road alone in the middle of winter.

He passes me without a second glance, and I drop my hand to my side. Damn it, what am I going to do? This road looks like it's hundreds of miles long. I'll die out here.

The sound of brakes has me lifting my head. Red taillights stare at me and the truck starts to reverse. Another high-pitched squeal leaves the truck, and I want to throw my hands over my ears, but I don't want to be rude.

The beat-up truck comes to a stop. Half the Chevy emblem on the fender is missing. The tan paint has faded in certain places, and the exhaust bumbles, dripping gasoline and black smoke. The silver handle is rusted, and the man driving leans across the passenger seat and rolls down the window.

That squeaks, too.

Jesus, this truck needs to be dipped and bathed in WD-40.

"What's a pretty thang like you doin' out here all 'lone?" he asks, throwing an arm over the passenger street.

"Just looking for a lift to the next town," I say, explaining myself as much as I can without giving the entire story away. Keep it brief. Keep it simple. It's no one's business but my own.

"I'm headin' out toward Henderson, if you want a lift." He opens the passenger side door and pushes it open with his hand.

Go figure, the hinges squeak too.

"Climb on in, pretty. I'll take you wherever you want to go."

I give him a bright smile and grab the handle to help myself in. "Thank you so much. It's so kind of you to stop." I bend to the right and pull the door shut, then roll up the window since it's so cold outside.

"Well, I wouldn't be a gentleman if I didn't stop to help a beautiful woman like yourself," he replies, grinning. He isn't the best-looking man in the world. He has on worn jeans with black spots, probably oil. His nails are dirty too, filled with the same dark soot, and his salt and pepper hair is sparse, greasy, and slicked back. His tank top is stained yellow with brown spots, and his chest hair curls over the top of the neckline.

His teeth are yellow with black in-between and his eyes drop to my chest, then my legs, and I pull the hem of Zain's shirt down to cover my thighs. "Let's get going, then." He yanks the gear stick down and presses on the gas. The engine gurgles before the truck lurches forward.

This wasn't a good idea.

I slide across the torn and cracked leather seat until my right side is pressed against the door. A heavy weight presses against my lower abdomen, as if I swallowed a ten-pound weight. I hold my breath when he reaches over the middle, then twists the knob of the volume button. "Let's get some music going. Sorry, ain't used to havin' company," he explains with too much excitement.

"It's alright," I say, twisting my hands in my lap.

Static booms in the speakers as he twists the knob that controls the needle to find a station. Music finally enters the cab, and he slaps his thigh when a banjo sounds.

The national anthem of hillbilly fate.

Damn it.

It's a bumpy ride in the truck that's been around longer than I have been alive.

The mountains are different sizes as we pass them by. My right leg shakes, and I pinch my lips between my fingers while staring out the window. My nerves are getting worse, my stomach knotting, and my instincts warning me that I need to jump out of this moving vehicle if I have any chance of survival.

The truck slows down, right before the Henderson sign, and he pulls off the side of the road.

I begin to tremble, and I continue to stare out at the desert. If I look at him, I'm afraid of what will happen. His hand lands on my thigh and inches up until I squeeze my thighs together. Tears pool to block my vision, causing the desert to look like it's underwater.

"Aw, come on, now, blondie. You know you gotta pay me back for givin' ya a ride. What'd ya expect?" he says, his lips too close my ear and his breath heating my cheek.

LUNATIC

It smells of old chewing tobacco and morning breath.

I hold a hand over my mouth to stop myself from throwing up.

"Now, why don't you lay back and spread those thighs. Pay up."

I slap his hand, then backhand him across the face. "You won't touch me," I hiss.

He grabs me by the back of the neck, then punches me in the face with the other. "I'm gonna do whatever the fuck I want to you. I'm going to fuck your face, your cunt, and your ass. Then, I'm going to toss your naked body on the side of the road while you're dripping of my come and let the buzzards have ya." He grips my shoulders and forces me to lay flat against the seat.

"No! Get off me!" I scream, but he shoves his filthy hand over my mouth. I can taste his sweat on my tongue and a hot tear sears my cheek while he pulls up my shirt and tries to yank my shorts down.

I'm not going down without a fight.

With a deep breath, I lift my knee, slamming it against his gut. He groans in pain, but I'm far from done. I slam my head against his nose and blood spurts out, dripping down his chin. "You fuckin' bitch!" he screams. "You broke my fucking nose!"

"And you messed with the wrong bitch, you disgusting fuck," I exclaim, then reach down and grab his pathetic dick. "This is what you wanted, right?" I squeeze and squeeze, then pull until he is crying out in pain. I twist, which has him doubling over and gagging. "You should have thought twice.

Don't you know not to pick up hitchhikers off the side of the road?" I sit up and pull my shirt down, annoyed that the only time Chloe has use for me is when she's too weak to handle her own business.

He lunges for me again, and I dodge out of the way, then move to the driver's side. He has his back turned to me still, and before he can try to make a move again, I grab him by the neck and slam his face against the door. "How many women have you done this to?"

I lift his head again and use all my weight and smash the worthless thing against the window. The glass cracks and blood spreads along the broken slivers.

I smash his head again.

And again.

Until I'm heaving and sweating.

"How about I leave your body out for the buzzards? Huh? Tell me," I growl, snapping his head back by the grip I have on his thin patch of hair. He has glass in his cheeks and forehead and he's sobbing just like the pathetic loser that he is.

"Please," he begs. "Please don't do this."

"You didn't listen to Chloe when she said get off. Why would I do the same for you?" I open the passenger's side door to dump his body but think better of it when I think about what Zain and them bikers would do to him.

Or maybe I should kill him off.

They can help me bury the body, and I know Zain would help.

It'll take time, but Chloe will come around. The one thing she wants more than anything is to be loved.

Zain and us, we're a match made in fucked-up heaven. And there is no way in hell I'm going to let Chloe ruin that for me.

For us.

I climb in the driver's seat and push the fat ass's legs off the bench seat. "Get the fuck out of my way, you sorry piece of shit. Do you have cigarettes?" I ask him, but he doesn't answer. He's too busy coughing and choking on blood. "I know you have to." I reach into the glove compartment and push his belongings around.

I find a gun instead.

Oh, this just got a lot more interesting.

And the road to hell just got a whole lot shorter.

CHAPTER NINE

Zain

I STARE AT THE EMPTY SIDE OF THE BED. THE SHEETS ARE COLD, which mean she hasn't been in bed for a while now.

Cracking my neck, I try to take long, deep breaths. I try to calm down, but anger unlike anything I've ever felt before runs through my veins. Anger, fear, panic, everything hits me all at once.

I can't fucking breathe.

Why would she leave me? Why?

I pick up the mattress, gripping it as tight as I can and tossing it off the box spring. The bed slumps against the wall. It's nowhere near enough to make me feel better. It's too much. I grip the sides of my head and roar, then fling my arm out to throw the lamp off the nightstand.

The bedroom door kicks in and Reaper is there with helmet hair. "Now, Zain. Calm down—"

In two stomps I have Reaper by the cut. I pick him up and slam him against the wall. "Where is she?" I yell so loud my voice breaks and my throat becomes dry. "Where is Chloe? Where is Jessica? Where are they?" I scream into his ear. I hope it fucking bleeds. "What did you do to her? I'll fucking kill you," I threaten him, not giving a fuck that he is my nephew. If he is keeping her from me, so help me god, I will snap his neck right here.

"Put him down before I blow your fucking brains out," Knives snaps, cocking the gun he has in his hand and placing the barrel right against my temple. "I'll fucking kill you, you crazy fuck."

I don't blink. I don't flinch. I take my free hand and smack the gun away from me, then punch Knives in the face. He smacks against the wall, unconscious, and the gun clatters against the floor. It goes off, a loud gunshot ringing the air. A hole in the wall appears next to Reaper's head. He doesn't even flinch.

"Tell me where she is," I growl, on the verge of madness.

"She left. We tried to look for her, but we couldn't find her, Uncle Zain."

She left. Willingly.

Today we were supposed to get married.

I let go of Reaper's cut and he tugs the leather to get the wrinkles out. "What the fuck, Uncle Zain?"

My vision blurs and my world tilts. I let out an agonizing roar. It's as if my heart has been ripped from my chest. "Where. Is. She?" I scream, punching the wall with my fist and head out the door. "Where is she?!" I shout at the top of my lungs, hitting the walls with my fist as I walk down the hallway. I stomp the floor, sending loud, booming echoes all through the building.

"Where are they? Someone tell me! I have to find her. I have to. We were getting married today. She wouldn't leave me." I check the couch, but Oli, Zipper, Felix, and Goldie are lying there.

"I met her. She wanted to leave, Zain," Oli says as he picks up the TV remote. "She said she was leaving for you."

No. No. No.

"I have to find her," I mutter, barely able to get my thoughts in order, they're racing so fast. I lick the sweat off my top lip and close my eyes, trying to calm down, but it's pointless. I can't. I don't bother unlocking the door. I break the knob and fling it open so hard that the wood cracks when it smacks against the wall.

"Uncle Zain, you need to calm down. We will find her and bring her back."

"No! I need her now. I need her." The shout that leaves me is one of desperation and agony... damn it... the agony, it fucking hurts.

Why does it hurt so much when the love has been quick? Don't things like this take time? When the person leaves after a certain amount of time, isn't that when it is supposed to be painful? Not like this. I can't breathe like this.

"Uncle Zain—" Reaper's hand lands on my shoulder.

"Don't touch me," I grit. "Don't fucking touch me!" I roar the last word with every ounce of air I have left in my lungs, shrugging away his unwelcome compassion. "Why did you let her go? Why?"

"Uncle Zain." Reaper stares at me with pity, his eyes frowning at the ends.

I don't want pity.

I want Chloe. I want Jessica.

I want my women.

"You will go…" I begin to try to think of a plan, but I know it's not going to work. "We need to, I need to… damn it. I need think. Let me think. I just need to…" I wipe my forehead against my shirt to get the sweat off my brows, so it doesn't get into my eyes.

"Okay, Zain." Tool yanks my arms behind me. "I think we need to put you somewhere safe."

"No! Let me go." I fight him, tugging my arms from his hold. He's a strong fucker, which surprises me, since I'm so much bigger than him. I shouldn't be struggling, but I'm tired. I'm not all here right now. I'm lost in my mind. "Let me go. I need to find her. Please, let me find her." I kick and pull, shouting until my voice is raw, and I can taste blood in my throat. "She made me better." I struggle against Tool's hold, but I can't get out. And then Reaper throws his fist through the air. His knuckles connect with the side of my head, knocking the wind out of me.

They take the moment of weakness and use it their advantage, dragging me across the home.

"Oh, Zain," I hear Goldie in the distance somewhere.

I shake my head and sweat flings in every direction. I can't see anything.

Just. Static.

Zipper wraps an arm around Goldie, but no one does anything to stop them. I can hardly lift my head from the dizziness and pressure in my head.

"This is bad. This is bad. This is bad. 1, 2, 3. 1, 2, 3. 1, 2, 3." Oli is stressed. He only counts out loud when he is stressed.

A door opens and my feet thud down each step as Tool drags me. The basement is dark, wet, and reminds me of what the old mental institution looked like.

Small rectangular windows, the grime as thick as alligator skin and flickering lights that we have yet to fix.

The basement is our last project. We didn't think anyone would be down here. It's not livable. It smells musty, and I swear there is a scurrying of nails against the cement floor. My feet stumble across a puddle of stagnant water, splashing my ankles.

I'll need to figure out where the water leak is.

My head bobs as Reaper opens one of the doors to the padded room. The metal that makes them is rusted, and the screws and bolts that makes this a horror show are stripped and ruined. Reaper has to grunt, push, and give it his all to get the rust off the hinges.

"I hate to do this to you," Tool says, pushing me harder than necessary into the room. "You need to cool down."

I stumble, the pads on the floors still squishy even after so many years. I hit the nearest wall and watch my nephew push the door shut. This time, it's quicker with Tool's help. The moans of the hinges remind me of a woman back in the mental institution.

Groaning Gretel.

Apparently, she had too many electroshock therapies, and her speech had turned to complete mush. She could only groan.

And now she haunts me in my own home.

"I'm sorry, Uncle Zain," Reaper says as he shuts the door, sliding the lock into place. The light comes on next, but I don't look at the state of the room. I know it's shit.

I stare at Reaper through the glass circle on the door. That anger hits me again, getting rid of the dizziness I felt from being hit in the face. It's loud and fucking mean, tearing my soul in half when I see the only family I have left stabbing me in the back. Again.

I'm a pissed off bull and Reaper is my target.

Sprinting toward the door, I bellow an agonizing cry for the walls to remember for a later date, maybe they will sing it back to me. The metal hits my shoulder, but I'm too angry to stop.

"Let me out!" I back away until I'm far enough for decent speed, drop my shoulder, and run again. The door doesn't budge. There is a pad on the inside of the door softening my blow, but it still hurts. My shoulder throbs.

I lay my palm flat against the door, sparks flying across my skin with energy, fury, and sorrow. I lean my forehead against the glass and roll my head side to side. "Let me out, Reaper. She needs me," I explain, gasping for breath. "She isn't safe out there all alone. Please, let me out."

"I can't do that, Uncle Zain. You aren't in control."

I lift my head and meet his brown eyes through the glass.

I'm surprised to see they are full of tears like mine. "Please," I beg him, curling my fingers into my palm to make a fist. "I need her. I need her so much. Reaper, I'll do anything."

"I need you to gather your head," he replies, clearing his throat. With a shake of his head, his eyes are back to normal. My nephew is gone and in his place is the President of the Ruthless Kings. "You're a danger to us, to your friends, and if we find her—"

"—I'd never hurt her!" I slam my fists against the door, wishing it was his face. "I love her. I love her like you love Sarah. Please, I need to find her. They can't survive alone."

"I'll keep you updated," Reaper says.

I rear back and smack the glass with my forehead, but the damn glass doesn't crack. I keep doing it, damn the pain, while smacking my body against the door. I want it to break. I need something to break.

But the only thing breaking is me.

I'm not sure how long I do that for, but blood trickles down the bridge of my nose, my knuckles bleed, and I'm getting tired. I finally come to a stop, defeated, and watch the raggedy material on the floor soak up the sweat dripping off me in buckets. "Like father, like son," I mutter between breaths. "You're just like him."

"Uncle Zain—"

"—You are giving up on me just like he did! You're throwing me away because you don't understand me. You are putting me in a room that I can't get out of! You're just like him." I sag against the wall, spent and worthless just like I've always been.

"No, Uncle Zain, I'm not leaving you in here. It's temporary—"

"—Everything is temporary, but my madness is forever. I might not be able to count on much, but I can count on that. You've never been my nephew. My family. All they ever were was temporary. Get the fuck out," I say, hitting the door with my sore hand one last time for good measure. "Go another thirty-five years without me. You'll be fine."

Everyone always is.

"I'm not leaving," Reaper says from the other side of the door. His words are broken. He almost sounds like he cares. Or maybe my words hurt him, I don't know. I don't want to care.

The pads are soft against the back of my head, which feels nice considering what I've done to the front of it. I don't answer Reaper. I'm too fucking tired. Look around the room now, and I'm surprised to see that it's still in decent condition. The pads are no longer white, but an off grey from dust.

There is a wheelchair in the corner. It's rusted, and the leather seat has fallen in. It's nothing but bones waiting to be turned to damn dust.

I never thought I'd be able to relate to a wheelchair, but here I am.

"Uncle Zain—"

"—Just go, Reaper," I snap, the carelessness etched in every word I speak. "I didn't need anyone for the last thirty-five years, I don't need anyone now."

It's a lie.

There is no way in hell I can go another day like I did at the institution. My life was barren, cold, and alone. Now, it's full of chaos and love.

I've never have had a full life before. It's always been empty.

I guess this is what happens when a mad man dreams.

He finds himself in the same box he started out in.

CHAPTER TEN

Jessica

"God, you're pathetic. Will you stop moaning before I put a bullet in your head?" I tell the guy that tried to rape Chloe, me, us, whatever. We don't even know his name. I don't care enough to ask.

"I need a hospital," he sputters through a stream of blood running down his face.

"Yeah, you should have thought of that before you thought you could rape someone for the hell of it," I say, making a sudden right down the dirt road where I think the Asylum is. I don't know where else to go. I don't know what the fuck Chloe was thinking leaving like she did, but she's always been a little bitch about certain things.

Like fighting for what she wants.

I always have to do it.

The guy next to me moves and I cock the gun. "I'm not afraid to blow your damn brains out, perv. Don't move."

He whimpers and curls in on himself and starts to cry. I lift my nose when I smell something pungent.

I roll down the window by cranking the handle near the speaker on the door and gag. "Did you just piss? You did. God, you're disgusting." The truck dips and squeaks, and I'm worried a tire is going to break off and send us rolling to our side. Does that happen? I'm pretty sure it happens.

The Asylum is less than a half mile from the road. No real path leading to it besides tire tracks through the desert.

"Please take us back," I whisper, hoping Chloe didn't ruin this for us. This is our chance to be accepted and loved. The one thing we have always wanted and have never been able to receive because of how different we are.

He has to take us back.

Please.

We need him.

Four bikes, two trucks, and a Lincoln Continental.

The Asylum is a beacon for me, calling out my name to bring me home. There are areas that are missing chunks of brick since it hasn't been fixed yet. Some of the windows are still broken or cracked. The roof is new, and the porch hasn't been stained yet, but I can imagine having sweet tea on a rocking chair, staring out toward the mountains, and holding Zain's hand.

I hope they don't change too much of what the

Asylum originally looks like. It needs to reflect the people living in it.

Lost.

Stricken.

And undoubtedly beautiful.

I slam the truck into park and turn off the engine, tucking the keys in my pocket so this asshole doesn't get any ideas. I open the door and slam it shut. I notice blood at the hem of Zain's shirt, and that just pisses me off more.

I loved this shirt.

Biting the inside of my cheek, I stomp around the front of the truck and yank the passenger's side door open. The perv falls to ground and sand sticks to his bloody shirt and face. I grab him by his arm and try to drag him, but he is too heavy.

"For a perv, you're a doughy fuck," I grunt, moving less than an inch before I give up. "Hey!" I yell at the house, hoping someone hears me, but the door remains shut. "Oh, for fuck's sake," I mutter, impatient and hungry. I could go for a steak, maybe some eggs. Oh, yeah. That sounds good. I lift the gun in the air so I can get on with my day and fire, the loud shot piercing the air.

My hostage screams on the ground and curls into a ball.

"Oh, stop. I haven't shot you." Yet.

The door slams open and the biker with all the tattoos and a screwdriver behind his ear stands on the front porch. "Well, reckless endangerment came back," he notes. Then he sees the man on the ground and his shoulders sag. "Who the fuck is that?"

"Oh, him?" I ask, tucking the gun in the waistband of my pants. "That's the guy that tried to rape Chloe. But have no fear, Jessica is here." I place my hands on my hips and puff out my chest like a superhero.

"Oh my god, are you—is she—are you both okay?" Tool tries to figure out how to address me. It's actually kinda cute. I appreciate the effort.

"Oh, yeah. We are golden," I grin.

Out of the corner of my eye, I see the perv trying to crawl away and my patience snaps like a thin twig. "So I'm going to need help, Tool."

He pounds down the steps and slowly walks next to the stranger as he crawls, digging his fingers into the desert. "With what? Want us to torture him? It's been a while. I think the boys back at the clubhouse would like that," Tool says, squatting next to the man's head. Tool kicks the guy to his back and lays a boot on his neck, cutting off his air supply. "My friend Tongue has been dying for some fresh meat."

"Great. I'll leave you two to get to know each other, then. I'm going to go see Zain. I have some explaining to do about Chloe's actions." I tuck my hands in my back pockets and head toward the steps, thinking about what I'm going to tell Zain. Maybe I won't tell him anything. I'll just lay a kiss on him and drop to my knees.

"About Zain…"

Stopping mid-step, foot hanging in the air, I turn around and grab onto the rail.

Tool knocks the perv out in one swift and hard punch,

rendering him unconscious. He picks him up and throws him in the back of a truck, carelessly.

"What about him?" I snap when Tool decides to take forever to tell me. I feel myself shrinking back. Chloe wants to take over, but I don't want to let her. I don't trust her to stay.

"He went a little crazy when he figured out you left. We had to put him downstairs in one of the padded rooms. He isn't okay."

Knowing he isn't okay sends Chloe pushing against me so strong that I don't have a chance to fight her off.

"What happened?" I ask Tool, who is kicking dirt over a pool of blood. The truck that stopped for me is here but the man that tried to… I hold a hand over my mouth and gag. "How did I get here?"

"Chloe? I was talking to Jessica?" Tool asks, stunned, then climbs onto the back of a truck.

"You couldn't tell?" I'm offended. I'm nothing like her.

"She said this man—" he lifts the guy's bloody head up so I can see him, "—tried to get handsy with you. She kicked his ass and brought you guys back here. I'm taking him to the clubhouse. Zain is downstairs because he flipped his fucking shit when he found out you were gone. There. That catches us up."

"Help me!"

"No one is helping you, you sick fuck." Tool slams the guy's head into the side of the truck and wipes his hands as if it's all in a day's work.

"Zain is locked away? How could you do that to him!"

I yell, debating if I want to shoot Tool for throwing Zain in a room like trash. I'm not the killing type. I doubt I could do it, but right now I wish I could.

Tool laughs and jumps down from the truck, his big black leather boots kicking up dust. "Oh, don't act high and mighty with me. You're the one who left him, remember?" he says, wiping his hands on his jeans. "Tell Reaper what happened. He's downstairs with Zain. I'll be back after I drop this asshole off."

I don't wait for Tool to rip out of the parking lot. I spin on my bare foot, something I really need to stop doing, and run up the steps. When I get inside, Goldie is crying, Zipper is holding her, Oli is counting, Felix is swatting the air, and the one in the toga must be Apollo.

"This is bad. Bad. Bad. Bad, Chloe!" Oli yells at me.

"I'm sorry," I sob, feeling more guilty than they will ever know. "Please, tell me where he is."

"No. No. No! Not if you leave again. 1, 2, 3. 1,2, 3. 1, 2, 3," he chants, counting on his fingers.

"I'm not going to leave again. I swear. Please." But Oli is too stressed out to give me his full attention.

"He is downstairs," Apollo states, flipping a page of a book. His legs are crossed, and he looks regal and important. "Where I come from, they aren't afraid to execute people for betrayal. You'll keep that in mind, won't you, Chloe?"

As if I can forget a threat like that.

I don't bother talking to them anymore. I hurry down the hall and see Zain's door open. Maybe they brought him back upstairs. I skid to a stop and I'm taken aback when I see the destruction. The bed is tossed on the floor, the lamp is broken, there is a hole in the wall.

And blood.

But whose?

Weak in the knees, I nearly collapse, but hold myself up on the wall and use it as a crutch to get to the next door I see.

It's locked.

"No!" I cry, hating that I don't know this house like the back of my hand.

I jiggle the next handle and the next. I feel like I'm in one of those fun houses with different sized mirrors that give the illusion you're lost.

When I grab the next handle, it turns and opens. Cold air hits my face, and a broken stairwell vanishes into the depth of darkness in the basement. The void seems never-ending. I know I'm in the right place.

"Uncle Zain, you have to stop. You're going to hurt yourself."

Bang. Bang. Bang.

Reaper's voice has me rushing down the stairs, almost tripping since I can't see.

Bang. Bang. Bang.

"Let me out! I need her," Zain's voice is raw and emotional, piercing my heart with another wave of guilt.

The only light on is one above Reaper. It's a pale-yellow light, barely casting a glow across the floor. There is a bright white light in the room Zain is in that's shining through the circular glass, casting a reflection on the wet floor. Reaper has his back against the wall, his head in his hands.

"Uncle Zain, please stop. You're going to hurt yourself. I'll get the straitjacket if I have to, if it means it keeps you safe." Reaper rubs the heel of his palms in his eyes as Zain continues to torment the metal door.

Bang. Bang. Bang.

"Let. Me. Out!" Zain roars, smashing against the metal door again. There is blood smeared on the glass and floors shake every time Zain connects with the metal.

The water on the floor ripples and it helps me peel my feet off the floor. "Let me in!" I tell Reaper.

"Chloe? Chloe? Is that you?" Zain appears in the glass. His forehead has a cut on it and his lip is busted.

"Zain, what did you do?" the words shake as they leave me. I hold up my hand to the glass and Zain does the same.

"I can't let you go in there, Chloe. I'm sorry. He is too dangerous."

"He won't hurt me, Reaper."

"I was only trying to get to you," Zain says. "You came back." He sags against the door, still thumping it with his head. "Thank you for coming back to me."

I don't think I stood a chance at leaving. "I'll never leave again. I promise."

"Why did you leave?" His shoulders heave as his arms cage his head as he reaches to the top of the door.

And he sounds fucking pissed.

"Why. Did. You. Leave!" He spews spit against the glass as he shouts, his voice echoing off the walls.

"Let me in," I whisper to Reaper.

"No. I'm afraid you won't come out."

"I don't care."

Reaper stands there, exhausted, the bottoms of his jeans wet, and his hair messy from running his fingers through it too much. "Fine. It's your fucking funeral."

"And as long as you bury me with him, I'll be happy."

He unlocks the door once Zain has stepped away from the opening, and throws it open, metal grinding against metal. He shoves me inside just as Zain charges and the lock slides into place, trapping me inside with mania.

And Zain doesn't slow down.

I don't have time to scream before his arms wrap around me in a tight, punishing hold as he straps me to his chest. He slams me against the wall, his eyes glowing that sinful garnet as he glares at me. "Why did you leave? I told you," he leans his forehead against mine, "I told you you'd be locked away." His hands wrap around the base of my neck and press me harder against the pads. "I was serious. You are mine. Do you understand?"

"I understand, Zain. I left because I didn't want to be a symptom of your mania. I didn't want you to regret me."

His brows pinch and pain stretches across his face as if my words inflict pain. "I could never regret you, but I am mad at you. I'm fucking furious that you think you could ever be a symptom when you make me feel like this…" He rocks his pelvis against me, and the hard, wide ridge of his cock presses against me. "Do you feel that Chloe? Do feel what you do to me? I've never felt that a day in my life with anyone else. You might make me insane, but I've never felt saner than I am when I'm with you."

This is usually when I push him away, or fight the need I have for him, because I don't know what I'm doing. After what almost happened in that man's truck, I know the time and place. I know the person. It's Zain. He's meant for me.

I can't be afraid anymore.

Not when my two halves finally feel whole.

"I'm so fucking mad at you," he sneers, tilting his head left and right as he debates giving me a kiss. "I want to bend you over, spank you so hard you beg for me to stop while I fuck that cunt. I want to own you, claim you, and when you're tired, dripping of my come—" he licks a path up my neck, over my chin, and bites my lip, "and begging me to stop," Zain places his mouth next to my ear. "I'm not going to stop. I'm going to fuck your face, your ass, and your pussy until all you see, taste, and feel is me." His nails dig into my neck and he drags them down, leaving behind a slight burn.

My eyes roll to the back of my head. He keeps dragging his nails down until his palms cup my breasts. My nipples are hard. My panties are drenched, and my hole is pulsating and aching to be filled.

"Zain," I whisper.

"Are you afraid of me?" he asks.

I should be. The dried blood on his face in frightening, but it doesn't scare me because I know it's only there for me.

I shake my head.

"You should be," he growls, sending my nipples into a tight frenzy. "Because you have no idea what I want to do to you."

"You won't hurt me," I say.

He closes his eyes and inhales, rolling his head back onto his shoulders. "Oh, but I want to, Chloe." He grips the shirt I'm wearing at the collar and tears the material down the middle like it's paper. The pajama top shows underneath and he sneers at it with hatred. He pulls the lapels of each side and rips the buttons off until I'm bare.

He flings the scraps of material off my body, then yanks my shorts down. The air breezes over my tits, and I clutch my thighs together when my clit pulses.

"I want you to ache. I want you to hurt when I'm done with you. Maybe then you'll realize you can't leave me again." His fingers slide between my cleavage, then up again, cupping the back of my head. He throws me to the side, and I'm not expecting it. I fall to the padded ground, but it doesn't hurt. Zain stares down at me, a delusional man experiencing an episode and I'm caught right in the middle.

Surprisingly, I'm right where I want to be.

His round biceps flex when he reaches behind his neck, fists the collar of his shirt, and yanks it off. "You're fucking gorgeous," he admires me as I push to my hands and knees. "Those tits, that ass." He licks his lips. "Sit down and spread your legs. Let me see that pretty pink pussy," he says.

I don't move intentionally.

"I said sit up and spread your legs, Chloe!" he bellows, cracking his shirt in the air like a whip.

A snake of lust slithers down my spine and sinks its fangs into me from the order that resounds in the room.

A gush of liquid heat escapes me, so I spread my legs to show him what he does to me.

Like the good, sweet girl I am for him.

CHAPTER ELEVEN

Zain

I'm fucking furious and I'm going to take it out on her. She deserves it for leaving me the way she did. The panic I felt, the rejection, the despair, the undeniable heartbreak. She'll never leave me again. I won't allow it.

This room... yes... I'll leave her in this room forever. She can't leave me if there is no way for her to get out.

She made a mistake deciding to come into this room.

The man I was when she left isn't the same man standing in front of her.

I drop my pants when I see the nectar dripping from her cunt. The pink shining in the white light causes my mouth to water. My cock slaps against my stomach, a bead of precome sticking to my happy trail. I fist the aching flesh, feasting my eyes on her hourglass figure. Her tits are big, nipples bright pink, and there is light blonde patch of hair above her cunt. I want to tug on it, bury my nose in it, inhale her scent before I slip my tongue between her folds and taste what is mine.

"Touch yourself. I want to see you fuck your fingers. You aren't allowed to come."

She whimpers, sliding her hands down the golden sun-kissed flesh. Her fingers part her sheath, dipping her fingers inside that tight hole. The deeper she inserts her fingers, the wetter they get. I groan, my eyes rolling back when I think about my cock feeling her wet heat.

I fall to my knees, the pads giving from my weight, and I fuck my fist, squeezing my cock as tight as possible.

"Zain," she moans my name, arching her body while her free hand grips her tit. "It feels so good." Her hand moves quicker and the wet sounds of her inner muscles sucking in her fingers have me losing control. "I'm going to—"

I rip her hand away, gripping her wrist tightly. "I said you weren't allowed to come. You don't listen very well." My tongue licks her honey from her palm, then I bring those slender fingers to my nose, inhaling the sweet scent. I suck them into my mouth, rolling them over my tongue. "You're delicious."

"Zain, please. I'm sorry I left. I'll never hurt you again."

"Damn right you won't," I state, then flip her onto her stomach, lift her to her knees, and bring my hand down on her ass.

And it isn't a playful slap.

I don't want her to sit for a fucking week. I want it to hurt when she even thinks about getting comfortable, a reminder of the pain she made me feel in my mind and heart.

"Oh god!" she cries out, trying to dig her nails into the pads.

A red handprint shows up on the silk canvas of her ass, and a bead of sweat drips down the bridge of my nose and over my top lip. I drink the drop, letting it coat my parched throat, but it doesn't help, because the longer I stare at her peach ass with my handprint, the thirstier I become for her.

My hand comes down again with more force than last time, creating a new welt on her other cheek.

"Do it again, fucking do it! Hit me harder. Punish us!"

The malicious laugh escapes her, and I know I'm not dealing with Chloe anymore. She pushes her ass against my hand and moans, her skin hot to the touch. "Jessica, you're being greedy. I'm not going to give you what you want."

"Please, just one hard smack and I'll go away," she begs, the words caught on a moan.

"I'm not going to give you anything until Chloe and I settle this."

"Zain, please. I need you to," she begs on the verge of tears.

A small of amount of anger dissipates, and I bend over, giving Jessica a kiss on the bottom of her spine, just where the tailbone is. "It's not you I'm mad at, sweet girl. It's Chloe. You'll get yours; I promise."

"You swear?"

"On my fucking life." I bend over her body, my cock

sliding between her wet folds and over the bundle of swollen nerves. I cup my hand under her chin and tilt her head back, keeping a firm grip on her throat. Her lips part and I breathe into the space, giving her air, giving her the ability to fucking breathe, then slip my tongue between her lips.

Our lips move in a more urgent manner.

It feels like if we don't pour everything we have, everything we are, into this kiss, we will die.

"I swear," I whisper, pulling away from Jessica, breaking the most intense kiss of my life.

She whimpers, moving her pussy along my cock so the head bumps her clit. I growl, enjoying the feeling of her taking from me. A few seconds won't hurt. "I brought us home," she admits. "It was me. Please, let me come," she says, flipping the golden strands back, moving her hips quicker. Her lips hug my cock, keeping it wet and warm while she uses me, the crown rubbing over her most sensitive area.

I fist her hair and lift her up until her back is flush with my front. "You swear? Is that the truth?"

"I swear. I swear, Zain!"

"Good girl," I say, praising her for bringing her wayward half home. I thrust my hips quicker, faster, knowing that this is okay, because not only does she deserve to feel good, but I'm not taking Chloe's cherry.

Not until Jessica is satisfied.

"Yes. Oh, fuck yes, Zain. Faster! I want you to fuck me so bad. You can inflict all of your wicked ways on me. I'll love it. Please, fuck me," she begs, her pussy tempting me to the point where if I wasn't insane, she'd drive me to the fucking front row of it.

"No, and you know why," I say. It's important to me that the first time I have sex with Chloe, she's present. She's the original personality of this beautiful body and mind.

And it's her I need to show what happens when she leaves me.

Jessica's body tenses, and her arm tightens around my neck as she tries to climb up my body. Her nectar floods my cock as she tenses, leaning her head back onto my shoulder. My name leaves her lips in a seductive song that I could listen to on repeat all day. I reach down and squeeze my orbs until it hurts to stop my orgasm. I bite the inside of my cheek to hold in the sound of pain.

While I'm fucking furious at Chloe, I don't want this to end too soon.

"Promise?" Jessica whispers against my cheek, breathless and sweaty, the puffs caressing me like a feather.

Her skin bathes my fingertips in beads of sweat. The flesh is warm, silken, and flushed from her orgasm. My palms squeeze her tits coaxing another shutter within her bones. "On my life, sweet girl. On my fucking life." She turns around in my eyes and I witness Jessica fade away and Chloe emerge.

They are so easy to tell apart. There is always a frown in the middle of Chloe's brows, whereas in Jessica's, there is always a devious tilt in them, like she's up to no good.

"Zain." The way Chloe says my name has my sack pulling tight against my body and my resolve almost breaking.

She's closer to me now, her innocence engulfing me like fog after a storm. Her palms rest against my chest, her fingers drawing circles on my sternum. "I know Jessica is more of what you want—"

I slam my mouth on her before she has a time to say another word. I hold her head still, controlling the kiss so I can do whatever the fuck I want to her mouth. Our teeth click together, uncoordinated, and our tongues don't meet because I'm nearly fucking her throat with mine. I'm so fucking angry. If I could possess her body and let her know just how much her leaving affected me, I'd slide under her skin and own her soul, so she experiences every ounce of torment I felt.

"You fucking left me," I hiss, choking on my heightened emotion.

"I'm so sorry, Zain. I thought it was what was best at the time. I shouldn't have left."

"What's best is if you and I stay together. That is what is best."

"I know. I'm so sorry, my love," she says, the nickname nearly making me fall into her lap like a fucking puppy.

I have to hold my ground.

I lean my forehead against hers, close my eyes, and let the rage of being abandoned replace rationale.

On their own accord, my knees slide against the cushions lining the ground. My arm circles around her waist, and I slam her against the nearest wall. Her legs wrap around my hips and her nails dig into the back of my neck when she feels the tip of my cock at her entrance. She inhales a sharp breath, her hazel eyes swarming with insecurity, yet anticipation.

"Sorry isn't good enough." Without warning, without ease, I drive ten inches of wide, driven steel inside her, claiming her as mine.

She tosses her head back, a guttural moan catching in her throat.

I'm not gentle.

I don't wait for her to adjust.

I'm too fucking mad.

Her pussy is drenched and when I look down, her juices are coating my legs. It's like pouring kerosene on a wildfire.

Curling my arms over her shoulder to lock her pelvis to mine, I ram harder, groaning in pleasure as her velvet muscles ripple around me.

"Don't." Thrust. "Ever." Thrust. "Do. That. Again." I punctuate each word with a violent thrust of my hips and she's screaming my name so loud my ears ring.

She's meeting me thrust for thrust, her tits bouncing in rhythm as she fucks me in return. "I swear, I won't. I swear!" she promises, taking every inch of my cock like the sweet girl she is.

"You're going to marry me, goddamn it, you are. You will not deny us this." I flip her onto her stomach without pulling out, yank her arms behind her back, and hold onto them so tight. Her cheek rubs against the pads, no doubt where so many others have cried and screamed.

"I'm going to…I'm going…. Zain!"

I yank out of her so she doesn't come, and she whimpers, nearly sobbing in frustration. "No! Zain, why did you stop? Please, I hurt for you."

"I know," I say.

Because I ache for her too. But she isn't allowed to know that right now. I grab her wrists and sling her to the floor, pushing her onto her knees. Her ass is up, still red from my handprint, and her puckered hole winks at me.

Rutting my cock between her cheeks, I stare in fascination as her honey and my precome mix to become the perfect lubricant. She's all fucking mine.

"I need you. Please, don't stop. I need you." Chloe turns her face to the side and a tear drops down her cheek.

"Are you in pain?" I ask, chest heaving and heart breaking when I see she's crying.

"No," she says. "No, I feel so good, but I need you inside me. Take over me. I'm yours, Zain. I'm yours."

The way she says 'I'm yours' settles the beast in me that needed to feed off desperation.

"You're mine," I repeat in awe, rubbing a hand down her damp skin, slicken with salty drops of perspiration. I drop my forehead to her back and sigh, pressing a kiss directly between her shoulder blades.

She's salty and sweet, a delicious combination to match her personalities. I hum in appreciation, then gather her hair off her neck where it is sticking to the skin. I press kisses along her neck and gently turn her over.

I trace her face with my calloused fingers, every soft ridge, every shadow cast upon her face. I settle between her legs, my cock still hard as a rock and dying to be inside her, and we stare at each other.

In those quiet moments, with no sound but our heavy breathing, I learn everything about her eyes. Her lashes are long and curl at the tips. The iris has twenty shades of green and blues I swear the world hasn't thought of yet, with a hint of gold right around the pupil. One more tear falls from her bottom lash line and I kiss it away as I ease into her.

"I'm alive for you," she says.

"And I'd die for you, Chloe."

I quicken the pace, lift her right leg, and try to slide as deep as I can. I want to flood her body and possess it the only way I know how. "Chloe, you feel so good, sweet girl. This cunt was made for me."

"Yes. Just for you." She holds her big tits as they bounce from my brutal thrusts, not because I'm mad, but the way we are joined is intense.

She releases her tits and scratches down my back, causing me to arch.

I bite the curve of her neck, leaving indents in her skin.

She sucks my lip into her mouth.

I groan down her throat.

She doesn't tell me when she's about to come, not like Jessica, but I can sense it. Her whimpers are closer together, her movements sporadic, and her cunt becomes extra wet. She isn't saying anything, and she doesn't have to in order to make me feel like I've done my job as a man to please her. Her body is speaking for herself.

Those damn nails scrape down my back, right down to

my ass, and she tugs me toward her, sinking that last inch in her channel. Her muscles contract and squeeze, and the last groan that leaves her mouth has my orgasm working its way through my body. I feel it everywhere. My mind, my heart, my soul, my fucking toes, since they curl. I toss my head back and let out a noise that's between pleasure and pain.

Pain because it is so intense and feels so fucking good.

I come, planting myself in her depths, and with every thrust I try to get each spurt to reach farther than the last.

Looking down at her, her hair is spread around her head like a bright halo.

She's an angel fallen to a wicked heaven.

And her feathers shed as she descends from grace.

Grace being her old life.

The wicked heaven being me.

"I love you," I tell her, flipping us so I'm on my back and she's laying on top of me.

My cock is still hard and lodged inside her. She props her chin in her hand and grins, showing perfect white teeth. "I love you too. It's fast. You don't think it's too soon?"

"Not for us," I say, tucking a piece of hair behind her ear. Her cheeks are hot to the touch and I love it because I did that. I made her body temperature rise. "We aren't like other people. We feel differently from everyone else. We are more. In every way. We feel more. We love more. We hate more. Everything is more when it comes to people like us and it isn't often that two broken minds find each other to create one that's whole. I'm a lot of fucking things Chloe, but I'm not an idiot. I know what I feel."

LUNATIC

"Me too, Zain. God, me too." She throws her mouth onto mine again, moaning when she feels me rock into her from the bottom.

Something smacks against the door, and I hear a painful 'ow' being drawn out.

"Oh, shit. Sorry!" comes Reaper's voice. "I wanted to make sure everyone was okay. Everything seems fine."

"Reaper!" I growl his name in a way that tells him he better get the fuck out.

"I'm unlocking the door and leaving. I didn't see anything!" His boots pound up the steps, and I let out a breath of relief.

"Oh god," Chloe covers her face with her hands and falls to the side. "This did not just happen."

"Don't say that too loud, Apollo might hear you and I'm the only god allowed in your body," I nip her chin and grip her ass.

"You have a god complex now? I know a girl who can take you down a notch or two." She runs her fingers through my chest hair, but the way she says it has a knot turning in my stomach. She's sad.

"Hey, what's that for?" I ask, running a thumb under her watery eyes.

"Do you like her more than me? Jessica? Do you wish I was her, full, without Chloe?"

"No, I don't wish that. I love you. I love her. I wouldn't want one without the other, sweet girl."

"Really?" she begins to cry but does her best to hold it back.

"Really."

"I just wanted to make sure," she says through tearful laughter.

"You accept me in ways I don't accept myself, just like I do the same for you. That's what this is about. That is us." I decide to get us the fuck out of this room. Now that I'm not in the middle of losing my mind, I can think clearly. "Come on, let's get out of here and go to bed. I'm exhausted." I slide out of her and we groan in unison.

I already miss being inside her.

I lift her into my arms and cradle her close to my body. I don't care about being naked, but she is and that has got to change. I press my back against the door and push, swinging the heavy metal open. I shiver when I see my own blood on the glass and then the wheelchair in the corner, a haunted room with who knows how many ghosts.

"Me too. We need to call Tool, though." She yawns and places her head against my chest.

"Why?" I ask.

"Um, we will talk about it later. Let's go to bed." I grab a straitjacket from the closet and drape it over her, so no one will see her body when we get upstairs. I debate if this is the best place to keep Porter instead of the second level. He's been quiet ever since we moved him, and I don't know if that's good or bad, but I need to figure it out now that I have Chloe and Jessica here.

Each step creaks from my weight as I climb the staircase. I check left and right to make sure each way is clear before running to my bedroom. I kick the door shut, then curse when I see the bed thrown against the wall.

The only item in the room not touched is the navy-blue recliner in the corner. "Sweet girl, I have to fix the bed—" but when I look down, she's sound asleep.

I press a kiss to the top of her head and inhale her scent, the smell of pine lingering on her from my soap. She makes it smell better than it does in the bottle. "Holding you sounds better than the bed anyway," I whisper, careful not to wake her as I sit down in the recliner. I lean back, stretch out, then throw the straitjacket off her and replace it with the blanket on the back of the chair. I cover us, close my eyes, and get lost in a feeling I haven't felt in all my life.

Relief.

CHAPTER TWELVE

Chloe

"You're going to have to run that by me again," Zain says, sipping his morning coffee with the familiar fire and brimstone heating those eyes to glowing garnet. The kitchen light shines on top of his bald head. I just want to kiss it all over, but I know now isn't the time. Tool just called asking what we want to do with the man who almost raped me.

"Morning. Morning. Morning," Oli greets me through a yawn, rubbing his right eye with his fist. He slips by Zain and heads toward the coffee maker.

"Good morning, Oli," Zain glowers into his coffee mug, but doesn't look at Oli. He is staring me down, waiting for me to repeat what I said.

I pretend I don't notice him and stir the creamer in my coffee.

"Glad you're back, Chloe. Jessica? Jessloe? Chisseca?" he snickers at himself, and I can't help but to giggle too.

"Chloe right now," I say.

"Chloe is going to tell me what happened yesterday."

"I don't know details, Zain. Jessica—"

"Then I want to talk to Jessica. I don't want to hear it from Tool."

"That isn't how it works—" but I emerge forward when I hear Zain call out my name. The darkness becomes lighter and lighter until I see his face and Chloe is the one in the distance now. She got to have all the fun yesterday. It's my turn.

"You rang?" I tease, batting my eyelashes at him playfully.

He knows it's all an act. He knows I crave only what he can give me. Just like Chloe, I want his love.

"Hey, sweet girl," he smiles, and it makes me all warm and fuzzy knowing he is happy to see me.

It kind of makes me feel coy. I place my arms in my lap as he devours me with his eyes. I remember what happened between us last night and the familiar throb between my legs begins to pulsate. I wiggle on the stool and hold in a moan by pressing my lips together as my clit rubs against the chair.

Zain is beside me, moving my hair so my neck is exposed. He kisses me there, right below my ear, and I stretch my neck to give him more access. "How's my little rebel today?" he whispers in my ear. My skin comes alive with goosebumps. Zain's lip drags across my jaw, and he licks my mouth until I open, allowing his tongue to drag across mine.

My walls I protect myself with come down, and I allow him to take over, dominating me like I've always wanted. I want to submit to him. I want to follow his every command and let go of control.

I'm always the strong one, always the protector, always the one taking over when Chloe is too weak to. I want someone else to control me. I want to give up my strength for once and enjoy surrendering to someone more powerful than me.

"Tell me, little rebel, what happened yesterday?"

"Little rebel? What happened to sweet girl?" I ask, liking this nickname so much better.

"Oh, I think we both know you deserve your own nickname, and sweet girl does not suit you does it?" he taps the tip of my nose with his finger.

I want to squeal like a teenage girl, but I don't squeal, so I swallow the urge to jump up and down like cheerleader. "I love it," I say calmly, gazing into his eyes. I can't believe we found someone like Zain. What are the chances of him loving us both?

"Tell me what happened," he says again.

I blow out a breath and pick up the spoon on the small plate and dip it into my coffee mug. Stirring, I try and remember the first thing that happened between me and the man in the truck. "I came to in the truck while a man was trying to rape us. He said he wanted payment. I'm assuming Chloe hitchhiked and the wrong man picked her up. I saved her ass, like I always fucking do. He got handsy and I kicked his ass. I drove us back here and Tool came outside and took the guy to the clubhouse. Then Chloe took over. I didn't come back until—" I blush remember the orgasm he gave me by rubbing his cock over my clit.

"Until you came all over my cock like a good little rebel."

"Zain," I moan, tilting my head back, expecting him to kiss me, but his hand wraps around my throat, then squeezes.

"Don't ever put yourself in danger like that again, do you understand me?"

"I'm going to go hang out with Goldie and Zipper. See you guys later. Bye, bye, bye!" Oli bustles out of the kitchen and disappears down the hall.

"I'm so fucking proud of you for protecting what's mine, Jessica. It turns me on." He lifts me from the chair by my throat and brings his face to mine. "I'm so goddamn hard for you right now, thinking about you kicking that bastard's ass, protecting my cunt. Because it's my cock that belongs there and only mine. Isn't that right?"

"Yes," I moan as he sucks my bottom lip into his mouth and tugs to the point of pain.

"You should be rewarded," he says, tightening his grip.

I gasp, searching for air, and the constraint has my panties wet and my nipples tight and begging for attention. "Yes," I rasp, standing on my tiptoes to naturally get away for the hold so I can breathe, but I know I won't be able to.

"But I need to go to the clubhouse and take care of the man that wanted to hurt you."

"He can wait," I offer the option. "Can't he? Can't I get

on my knees and suck your cock instead? That sounds…" I swallow hard to coat my throat. "That sounds more fun, don't it?"

"It does, but I'm very pissed the fuck off, and want to kill him for touching you. For touching what's mine. And then when I'm done, I'll force you to your knees and fuck that pretty face until you gag, Jessica."

My eyes flutter shut at the thought.

"You like the idea of that, little rebel? You want me to stretch those lips wide until I hit the back of your throat?"

"Mmmhmm," I whine, remembering how big his cock felt rubbing my clit.

His hand moves to my left jaw and holds on tight. "Then, I'll fuck that tight pussy again, fill you up until you're dripping, then use our come to get your ass ready, and then I'll fuck you there too."

"Yes! Zain, please." Just the thought of him using me like that has me on the edge of orgasming, right here in the kitchen. If he keeps talking like that, I just might.

"But you expect me to turn a blind eye to the man that almost hurt you?"

"No," I disagree with him and reach out to cup his erection. "I expect you to satisfy me first before you. I'm not asking you to ignore him, because I want to watch what you decide to do, but I want to be the priority. The fucking asshole can wait."

Zain growls so deep it reminds me of a wolf, especially when he curls his lip as he looks at me. "You're a demanding thing, aren't you?" he says, chuckling ironically.

"Yes," I answer, keeping my chin held high. I know what I want.

And when I want something, I always find a way to get it.

Just as I am his, he is mine, and I will kill anyone that dares to threaten that.

Even him.

His hand skims up my cheek, then side of my head, brushing his fingers through the strands. His face softens briefly, but the moment of tenderness is gone once his palm grips onto the top of my skull and pushes me down to my knees. I'm face to face with outline of his cock pressing against the denim jeans.

I reach up to undo his pants. He fists my hair and starts to pull and walk away at the same time. My scalp burns, but it feels so fucking good.

"You want it rough, little rebel?"

I kick and scream, slapping his hands as he drags me down the hall. I slap his hands to try and get him to let go, but I hope he doesn't.

I don't really want him to.

"Oh dear," Goldie gasps, peeking he head out the door when she hears the commotion, then slams it shut.

Zain kicks open his bedroom door, then uses his strength to throw me through the entranceway. I slide across the floor and hit the side of the bed, tears of pain burning my eyes from the rough hold he had on me.

I fucking loved it.

And I want more.

He uses his foot to close the door and he stares at me while he unbuttons his pants, then he unzips. I see a thick patch of dark brown hair, and my mouth waters when I see the base of his erection.

"Get naked," he orders.

That won't take long, since I'm only in an oversized shirt and shorts. I yank the black shirt over my head, then tug the shorts down and kick them away. I watch as his nostrils flare as drags his eyes up and down my body. "I'm going to fuck those big tits too one day." He pulls his pants free. My eyes round and I suck my bottom lip into my mouth when his cock slaps against his stomach. The veins in the plump flesh are protruding, filled with blood that has his cock large and intimidating.

The plum-shaped head is purple, and there is a shiny drop leaking from his slit.

"Sit down on the edge of the bed." He points to the mattress, and I sit down eagerly, wanting to obey him as if it is encoded in the fibers of my DNA.

I watch him strut, his muscular thighs flexing, his ass firm, and his cock swinging. God, the man is a bear. I want him to ravage me. He bends down to pick up a white jacket off the floor and comes to my side. "Do you know what this is?" he asks.

I shake my head.

"It's a straitjacket. It's used to keep patients from using their arms, to contain them so they don't hurt themselves or others."

I gasp when he drapes it around me.

"Cross your arms."

I do as he says, and he zips the jacket from the base of my spine to the back of my neck, then tightens the straps. I try to move and a grip of panic washes over me when I can't.

I love it.

"I'll have to cut holes in the material later so next time I can see those big tits I love so much," he says, standing in front of me until his cock is nearly touching my cheek. His hands land on the back of my head, and the blanket under me gets wet from the desire dripping from me. "Suck my cock, little rebel. If you're good, I'll fuck you just how you want."

I'm going to suck him until his damn soul leaves his body.

I try to reach out and grab his cock with my hands, but the damn straitjacket stops me. It sends delicious waves of frustration and excitement through me as I open my mouth. He doesn't ease his cock into my mouth.

He thrusts into it, fucking my throat just like he promised.

His hips move quick. I gag and choke, coughing through it as he holds my head in my place while he uses me. Tears drip down my face, not from crying, but the natural reaction to gagging too much.

"Oh fuck yes," he groans.

I lift my eyes up to see him, and through the blur of tears, I can tell his head is tilted back.

"You like that? You like taking my cock down your throat?"

"Mmhmm," I try to say around the mouthful of dick.

"Yeah, you fucking do," he growls, hammering into my face to the point I can't catch my breath. His heavy sacks swings and slaps me under the chin. I wish could reach down and rub my clit. I'm so wet that I can feel the slick running down my thighs. "I'm going to come."

He holds my head down, my nose buried in his pubic hair, and he grunts as his seed jets from him. He pulls out and the warm spurts land on my chin and neck. "You look so pretty covered in my come," he says, stroking himself so every drop hits my face.

My jaws hurt. My cheeks are wet. My lips are numb. Spit is dripping from my mouth along with come as I try to catch my breath.

I want more.

He is still hard, and he pushes me down, flat against the bed, and lifts my legs on his shoulders. He holds them down, scoops his come off my face, coats my pussy lips, and then rams himself home.

"Zain!" I scream, fighting the straitjacket with every thrust he gives me. I want to rip it off me and scratch my nails down his back. I want to touch him, but I love being able not to at the same time. It's a sick and twisted desire I have inside me.

To be used and dominated, maybe even a little humiliated too.

As long as it is Zain doing it, I don't care what he does. Just as long as he never stops.

"Harder. More. Fucking give it to me, Zain."

"You're a slut for my cock, aren't you?"

"Yes."

"Only my cock."

"Only yours," I say. "You fill me up and stretch me out so good. It hurts."

"That's right. Your greedy cunt only gets fed by me," he says, then flips us over until I'm on top of him. "I bet you wish you could touch me." He digs his fingers into my hips and holds on tight, rocking me back and forth on him. My clit rubs against his pelvis. His cock is buried so deep, I swear I feel him in my throat.

I move the best I can since I can't use his chest for leverage with my hands. "You're so deep," I moan, bouncing on his cock faster.

His hand goes to my cheek while the other helps me rock quicker. He lifts his hand and gives me a slap across the cheek. Only four of his fingers connect. He doesn't hit me to the point of pain, just enough to give me that delicious sting.

"Fuck! Again," I beg, arching my back, when the slap has an orgasm brewing.

"You're everything I've ever wanted," he says, slapping me again. The burn feels good, feels right. My body is on fire. He isn't hitting me hard enough to bruise or anything, just enough to feed the sadistic beast inside me.

"I'm so close, my love," I tell him. I can feel the sweat gathering on my back and between my breasts. "Again. Do it again!" My voice carries through the room as I raise it with every word I speak. "But harder."

He doesn't question me. He doesn't stop fucking me. He takes what I want in stride.

This time, he backhands me, the taste of blood pooling in my mouth.

And that's all I need.

I come.

My orgasm crashes inside me like a tsunami. "Yes! Oh, god. I love your cock. So big. So good, Zain. Yes," I scream. I can feel my walls flex around him, trying to suck him deep.

He rolls me to my back and thrusts into me three times through my orgasm, before he comes, releasing his seed for my trembling walls to pull in.

Zain flops down and kisses me, long and passionately, then rolls me to unzip the jacket.

I fucking love that jacket.

"I love you," he says, placing a kiss on my shoulder. "I'd do anything for you and Chloe."

I flip over and bury my face in his chest, the hair scratching my cheek as I allow myself a moment of weakness and cry. I've never been loved before. I always thought I was unlovable. "I love you too."

Zain wraps his arms around me in a hug. Not like the restriction of the straitjacket, but the softest warmth I've ever felt. He plants a kiss on my forehead.

"I'll take care of you two forever, Jessica."

I lay my ear against his heart and close my eyes, happy for the first time in forever.

"Zain!" Reaper knocks on the door. "Hate to interrupt, but the cable guy is here and needs your signature.

I'm heading out with the guys. I need to go check on Knives from the concussion you gave him."

Zain grumbles. "I guess I need to apologize."

Reaper's boots fade and the front door slams shut in his departure.

"Let's get dressed, little rebel. And then I'll fix you breakfast, let the cable guy do what he needs to do, and then we go to the clubhouse to take care of that damn asshole who touched you."

Damn, Chloe and I are two very lucky ladies.

And it's a good thing I'm happy to share, or we would have a problem.

CHAPTER THIRTEEN

Chloe

Jessica vanished the moment Zain opened the front door, and for some reason, my jaw was killing me. I'll have to ask Zain what happened.

"Sorry about the wait," Zain says to the cable guy. He's younger, tall, blonde hair with a baby face. He's cute, but he doesn't compare to Zain.

"It's okay. Not a problem. I'm Tyler." He reaches a hand out and Zain shakes it. "Is this where you want the cable? Just this room and nowhere else?"

"Yes. I'm tired of watching movies in here every time," Zipper says, startling me in my seat. The coffee spills on my hand and I hiss in surprise. "I want options." He jumps over the back of the couch and lands on the cushion. Oli, Goldie, and Apollo—who is still wearing a toga—walk around the sofa and sit down.

"I'll be in and out of here in no time." Tyler walks across the living room and grabs a few tools from his tool belt and gets to work.

Zain comes back over to me and kisses me senseless, no doubt tasting the coffee lingering in my mouth since that's what I'm drinking.

"You feeling okay?" he asks.

"Why does my jaw hurt?" I make sure to lower my voice to a whisper. "Did you and Jessica…"

He clears his throat and nods. "You're okay with that, right? You know I love you both."

"No, absolutely. I'm fine with it. Are you kidding? Do you know how happy I am that I found someone who accepts both sides of me? But… why does my jaw hurt?"

Zain leans down and his lips tickle my ear. "She likes it rougher than you do, sweet girl."

"Oh," I say, leaning my hand against my cheek. My scalp hurts too, but that doesn't take a rocket scientist to figure out that's from hair pulling. "You liked it?"

"I loved it, just like I love being with you."

I grin, reaching for my coffee cup. "Good," I say. And it is. I'm not jealous or angry. I'm actually satisfied, and so is Jessica. I don't know how I know that, but I do. I just… feel it.

Fifteen minutes later, the cable is installed, and Tyler gives Zain the remote. "Alright. You're alright. You have all the channels—"

"—Wait. I only wanted basic," Zain says. "There's a mistake."

"Yeah, someone over at the Ruthless Kings paid for you to have 120 channels for the next year."

"Awesome! Holy shit, we can watch football. Do you know how long it's been since I've watched football?" Zipper says excitedly, bouncing on the couch cushion.

"Thank you, Tyler. Have a good day," Zain says.

"Bye. Bye. Bye." Oli adds three waves to his farewell and Tyler salutes us before heading out.

"Well." Zain flips the remote in his hand. "How about we see what's going on in the world before we go?"

"Where are we going?" Goldie sniffles.

"The clubhouse. I have business waiting for me there," Zain replies, no doubt leaving more questions in Goldie's mind.

Zain points the remote to the unusually large flat screen TV and turns it on. "Hell, I don't know what channel to go to." He keeps clicking until a news channel appears, and on the bottom left side it has a Nevada News logo.

"The news? Boring," Zipper says, then pretends to sleep by snoring.

"I just want to see what's going on. I haven't known anything in… well, a long time."

"Sorry, Zain. I didn't mean—"

"Zipper, it's fine. No hard feelings." Zain turns the volume up and a woman with brown hair, blue eyes, and too much makeup fills the screen.

She brings the mic to her mouth and smiles. "Hi, I'm Michelle Pope reporting live from North Las Vegas, where a brutal double homicide took place. A Dr. Randall

Washington and his wife Theresa were found dead this morning by Mr. Washington's mother, who grew concerned when she hadn't heard from her son in nearly four days. There are no suspects at this time, but police are active in their search for the killer. The police do not think this is an act of a serial killer, so there is no need to panic. We will keep you updated as information comes forward. I'm Michelle Pope reporting live, stay informed with Nevada News."

"Well, there you have it—" another woman fills the screen, but Zain changes the channel before she can finish her sentence.

"Well, that was fucking depressing," Zipper mumbles. "All caught up now?"

I sit there frozen, shocked, and forget to breathe. I lay my hand to my chest and think about the last time I saw my therapist. Who would do such a thing?

The man I loved.

The man who knew me better than I knew myself.

Four days ago

"I'll see you next week, Chloe. You're making great progress. I almost think we can cut it down to one day a week. You've really accepted Jessica, and you're doing well on your medication. I think it's time we see each other less." He smiles, happy at the thought of only seeing me once a week.

"Oh," I say with disappointment and heartbreak.

"Chloe, this is what we have been looking forward to for the last three years. This was the goal. Aren't you happy?"

"Of course, I am Dr. Washington." I close my eyes when he places his hand on my cheek. He does that a lot. He likes to touch me every chance he gets, but we have never crossed the line because he is my therapist.

Closer to the goal.

Oh. Oh! We are closer, because eventually I won't have to see him at all. I throw my arms around his neck and kiss his cheek. "Thank you so much. I can't wait until next week."

He pats my back and pushes me away. "Let me grab my briefcase. I'll walk you out. You were my last appointment for the day."

I tuck a piece of hair behind my ear and smile. "I'd like that very much."

He gives me a quick tilted grin and grabs his briefcase from the chair, then we walk out into the hallway. He closes the door and locks it. As we walk down the hall of his private practice, the floors echo our footsteps. The marble is polished, a rich black that reminds me of the night sky without stars.

"What are your plans for the night?" he asks, and my heart kicks up when I wonder if he is going to ask me out.

"I'm going to go to my apartment tonight, put in a movie, eat bad food and enjoy the night off from work." It isn't an important job. It's mindless work, but I can't have a job that challenges me too mentally, or Jessica likes to rear her head. I'm a file clerk. It's boring, and it's part time. My parents are wealthy and give me all the money I want, but I want to be on my own. It's too bad I'm too incapable of having a real job or I'd support myself fully.

I've been fired eight times for punching my bosses in the face.

It wasn't me.

It was Jessica.

"You?" I ask him as we head into the cold winter night. Our breaths fog the air, and they mix, swirling together as they rise to the sky.

"I have plans. I'm going out to dinner with a few friends." Dr. Washington is so handsome. He's taller, with thick hair that has an edge of silver to it, and round glasses that make him appear more intellectual than he already is. He has stubble on his jaw, but not a beard. I can tell he works out by how his shirt stretches across his chest.

"Sounds fun," I say in yearning, wishing he'd invite me.

How long are we going to dance around each other?

"Well, this is where I leave you," he says. "I'm meeting my friends at the other end of the street."

"Oh, okay. I'll see you next week. Have a good night," I say, hoping he leans in and gives me a kiss.

"Have a good night, Chloe. Be safe."

I'm disappointed when he doesn't even hug me goodbye. He walks away, leaving me staring at his back. I turn around and start to walk away, but then think, what if him and I accidentally run into one another at the restaurant? Then, he'll ask me to join him and his friends.

It's perfect.

I turn and look over my shoulder to see he is far enough away to know he won't be able to see me. I switch directions and head down the sidewalk, following him from a safe distance. The sidewalk is new, with no cracks, and the cars are parked on the side of the road by the parking meters. Crossing my arms to keep my torso warm, I pass a few dark alleys and toppled trashcans.

There is a homeless man sleeping on the ground, his dog cuddled up next to him. I reach into my purse and pull out a twenty-dollar bill. It's all I have on me. I bend down and tuck it into his shirt pocket. I hope he finds it. I pat the dog on the head. I wish I could do more to help them, but just because I have a large bank account doesn't mean I have access to it.

My parents made sure of that because of my condition, I can be impulsive and spend a lot of money if I want to. So mom and dad put a leash on me. I can't spend a single cent without their approval. And they never approve of anything.

I continue walking, keeping an eye on Dr. Washington as he comes to a stop in front of a Fat Jay's steakhouse. The sign is in neon blue and green, casting a glow on top of Dr. Washington's dark head of hair. I jump behind a parked car and hide myself when he turns around. I wait a few seconds, giving myself enough time until I know he is gone.

I stand up and wipe my butt off, then head toward the restaurant. I peek inside the glass, my breath causing it to fog, and I wipe it away. I hold my hand over my eyes and look for Dr. Washington. I scan the crowd of people and when I see him, I jump up and down. I go to knock on the window but stop short. My smile slips off my face when I see a beautiful woman stand up from the booth with a wide smile on her face.

She's gorgeous.

Red hair, blue dress, and big lips.

He looks just as happy to see her, because he leans in and does the one thing I've always wanted him to do.

He kisses her.

It isn't quick.

It's long and deep. He dips her over his knee and her long flaming hair nearly touches the floor.

I press my back against the glass so no one can see my face as I cry. The sobs that leave my chest are loud, and they hurt my throat. I wipe the tears and I notice black streaks on my hands. My mascara is running.

I thought he loved me, but it was all a lie. He didn't love me at all.

I close my eyes and take a deep breath, then exhale. When I lift my lids again, I'm fucking angry and want revenge.

No one does that to Chloe.

No one.

If he wants to play games, then check-fucking-mate.

Chloe is gone. The nice, level-headed, good girl is in the shadows, and her stronger half is here. How dare this man? I've only met him a few times, but I didn't like him at all. He thinks he knows everything about why Chloe is the way she is. It's because of him she has accepted me, but he is trying to fix her now and pretend as if I'm not here.

I'm not going anywhere.

This is my body as much as it is hers.

I run across the street in a nearby alley, feeling the urge to dance under the moonless sky. That's for another time and another place. I dip into the narrow alley and watch the man Chloe loves enjoy a night with another woman.

I don't know how long I stand there. Minutes. Hours. All I know is my feet fucking hurt in these boots, and it's getting colder the later it gets. Finally, after a bunch of laughs and a few drinks and steak, Dr. Washington pays the bill and helps the woman up. When they walk out of the restaurant, they are hand in hand, still laughing.

Are they laughing at Chloe? Is he talking about her? I follow them, keeping enough space between us that they can't feel anyone behind them.

But I'm there.

And I'm fucking pissed.

We pass a few Spanish style homes, some with personal gates, and some with sand as a lawn. He's a therapist, so he makes good money. That's why I'm not surprised when we come to his mini-mansion. It doesn't have a gate. The home is Spanish style as well, with big columns in the front. The door is large with black hinges and a reddish-brown stain with a glossy finish.

When they get to the front door, his hand lands on her ass, gripping it and pulling her to his body. They kiss, their tongues shining in the porch light.

LUNATIC

My body burns with rage when I feel Chloe banging against the veil between us.

No way in hell am I going to let her out.

I hide behind a truck parked on the side of the road and watch them devour each other as they stand on the doorstep. He slams her against the door, running his hand through her luscious hair. I can hear them moaning from the sidewalk as he aligns their bodies and rubs himself against her. He fumbles with the lock, and he must say something because she laughs.

He pushes her inside and slams the door.

I come around the back end of the truck and step on the sidewalk. Dr. Washington has a fence but it's small and black, more for decorative purposes than protective.

His mistake.

I hurry down the walkway and when I get to the door, I listen by placing my ear against it. I don't hear anything. I try the handle to see if he locked it in his hurry to get into the woman's pants.

It opens.

"Tsk, tsk, Dr. Washington." I sneak into the house and close the door quietly. A few bangs from upstairs tell me where they are, and a second later, I hear a loud moan. That bastard. I check out the house. It's plain. Nothing special, just like Dr. Washington. He's boring. The entire place is beige on beige, even the furniture.

I head down the hall, keeping my feet light, and find myself in the kitchen. I look around at the stainless-steel appliances and the oversized kitchen island with copper pots hanging above, until I find exactly what I'm looking for: the block of knives.

Don't mind if I do.

I grab the butcher knife, the biggest one there is, and my reflection shines back at me. I tilt my wrist when I think I see Chloe screaming at me in the metal, but with another flick, she's gone. It's just my mind playing tricks on me.

My feet are light as they carry me down the hall and toward the steps. I have no second thoughts as my hand lands on the rail. I climb the steps.

"Yes! Oh, baby. That feels so good. Harder," the woman gasps, as skin slaps loudly from the room on the right near the staircase.

"You feel so good," he says in return.

I peek to the dark room and can barely see the outline of their bodies. He flips her over and has her on top of him. Her small breasts bounce as she rocks against him, and his hand squeezes the meat of her ass.

On the inside, I swear I can feel Chloe breaking into pieces from witnessing this. It's a good thing she won't remember.

I tiptoe into the room. Their breathing gets faster as they chase their orgasms. I'm right behind her and as she tosses her head back in orgasm, I slice the knife across her throat. Blood spills in quick waterfalls down her chest.

Dr. Washington screams, and I hurry to his side as his slut gasps for life.

I lift the knife in the air and stab him in the chest. Over and over and over. "How could you!"

"Jessica," he coughs.

Wow. He knows us pretty well.

"Chloe would never," he stutters through a throat full of blood.

"Chloe loved you. She thought you loved her. We thought—and then you fuck this woman?"

Dr. Washington cries when he sees the woman slump over him, his cock no doubt still lodged inside her.

"Theresa!" he shouts as loud as he can, tears streaming down his face. "You killed my wife! You killed her!"

"You never said you were married," I say, ripping the knife from his chest so he bleeds out.

"I don't want people...patients..." he coughs. "To know...too dangerous."

"Hmm, I see. You still led her on. And for that..." I bring the sharp blade to his neck and slice, the gurgling of blood a song of sweet revenge.

I don't look back.

I leave them there. I don't call the police. I don't do anything, but I do take the weapon with me. Chloe and me, we will find a new future somewhere else. Someone will find Dr. Washington and his wife's body.

They won't know it's me, and they won't be able to find the murder weapon because it will be lost in the desert.

It will be my little secret. Because Chloe will never know.

LUNATIC PLAYLIST

DOWN WITH THE SICKNESS BY DISTURBED

SOUND OF SILENCE BY DISTURBED

CRAZY BITCH BY BUCKCHERRY

DIARY OF A MAD MAN BY OZZY OSBOURNE

PARANOID BY BLACK SABBATH

PSYCHO KILLER BY THE TALKING HEADS

WHERE IS MY MIND BY PIXIES

PSYCHOTIC BREAK BY JERRY CANTRELL

MADHOUSE BY ANTHRAX

CRAZY TRAIN BY OZZY OSBOURNE

ACKNOWLEDMENTS

To our Ruthless Readers that turned a basic Facebook group and made everyone feel like it home. Is it weird to say a Facebook group is a home maybe but we're weird so it's perfect for us and it makes our black hearts happy.

Give Me Books, as always thank you putting up with us and making sure our release was a success.

To all the bloggers and reviewers thank you for all your support.

Wander as always thank you for always being our rock.

Andrey as always thank you for all you do, you are such an amazing person, I doubt you give yourself enough credit because you're selfless like that. But it's what makes you who you are, and we love you for it.

Donna thanks for always being my soundboard. #BOOMERISDONNAS

Stacey at Champagne Book Design thanks for making our books so beautiful.

Instigator you're the greatest, all the foots down dammit.

Tiff thanks for putting up with me and being my sanity when the little I do have is gone.

Silla, thanks for all you do. I'll share my Reese with you.

Mom love you

Jeff 5 little words

ALSO BY K.L. SAVAGE

PREQUEL - REAPER'S RISE
BOOK ONE - REAPER
BOOK TWO - BOOMER
BOOK THREE - TOOL
BOOK FOUR - POODLE
BOOK FIVE - SKIRT
BOOK SIX - PIRATE
BOOK SEVEN - DOC
BOOK EIGHT - TONGUE
BOOK NINE – A RUTHLESS CHRISTMAS
BOOK TEN - KNIVES

OTHER BOOKS IN THE RUTHLESS KINGS SERIES
A RUTHLESS HALLOWEEN

RUTHLESS KINGS MC IS NOW ON AUDIBLE.

CLICK HERE TO JOIN RUTHLESS READERS AND GET THE LATEST UPDATES BEFORE ANYONE ELSE. OR VISIT AUTHORKLSAVAGE.COM OR STALK THEM AT THE SITES BELOW.

FACEBOOK | INSTAGRAM | RUTHLESS READERS
AMAZON | TWITTER | BOOKBUB | GOODREADS |
PINTEREST | WEBSITE

READING ORDER
PREQUEL - REAPER'S RISE
BOOK ONE - REAPER
BOOK TWO - BOOMER
BOOK THREE - TOOL
BOOK FOUR - POODLE
BOOK FIVE - SKIRT
BOOK SIX - PIRATE
A RUTHLESS HALLOWEEN
BOOK SEVEN - DOC
BOOK EIGHT - TONGUE
BOOK NINE - A RUTHLESS CHRISTMAS
BOOK TEN - KNIVES
BOOK ONE- LUNATIC

Made in the USA
Las Vegas, NV
13 December 2024

14066214R00098